T0158158

The Adventures
of
Zorax Zoomster

Shemar James

CONTENTS

Prologue ix

Part 1

Chapter 1   Zorax's Adventure Begins 1
Chapter 2   Prison Pals 23
Chapter 3   Spaceship Battle 34
Chapter 4   The Journey Continues 40
Chapter 5   King Zemus's Wicked Plot 53
Chapter 6   Welcome to Planet Zigger-Zap 60
Chapter 7   Captured Again 66
Chapter 8   Interplanetary Showdown 69
Chapter 9   Reunited 79

Part 2

Chapter 10   Jail Breakout 83
Chapter 11   Zillozooba 88
Chapter 12   Rescue Mission 96
Chapter 13   Zelius versus Zemus 103
Chapter 14   The Misty City of Zelabell 109
Chapter 15   Plan Back to Zeliustopeia 115
Chapter 16   Zeliustopeia War 121
Chapter 17   Zorgatopolis Celebration 128
Glossary 131

PROLOGUE

There were thirty planets in the Azzon Universe. The enormous planets only had small populations of living beings, but one of them was a mischievous creature named Dr. Zillozongo. He was a greedy scientist whose only desire was to become wealthy and famous. He spent his days studying the mysteries of space, always seeking priceless collectibles among the stars, asteroids, and moons.

Dr. Zillozongo had recently discovered that valuable diamonds and gems could be found inside random asteroids, but what the doctor did not figure out was that the precious crystals inside the floating boulders possessed hundreds of extraordinary powers. If the jewels were broken open, these powers could be distributed around the universe, spread by a gas-like chemical that was contained within the stone. The color of the gas that was released depended on the color of the mineral. If the magic diamond dust was inhaled, it could enter life forms and change their DNA—transforming them forever.

Dr. Zillozongo knew nothing about the secret, but the thought of finding enough treasures to make him one of the richest aliens around was enough to keep him on the lookout for massive asteroids—the bigger the better. In the beginning of the Zerca era—Dr. Zillozongo's greed, perseverance, and his enormous telescope led to his spotting a gigantic asteroid. It was the largest asteroid that had ever been seen in this Azzon cosmos.

Dr. Zillozongo enlisted two of his trusted scientist friends—who were just about as corrupt as he was—to help him explode the huge rock so they could retrieve the multitude of gems the scheming professor knew would be inside. The three daring doctors carefully wired a pack of dynamite to the asteroid and then backed away to what they thought was a safe distance. They didn't go far enough to risk losing any of the beautiful jewels.

When the rock detonated, the gems inside cracked open, releasing a magical mist. Unfortunately, Dr. Zillozongo and his friends were instantly obliterated by the explosion, having perhaps been a little too close to the asteroid. The mist swept right past their microscopic remains and began traveling across the universe. It moved across many galaxies, continuing to extend in measurement as it traveled through endless space. As it did, it penetrated the skin and minds and hearts of many living beings. These beings gained a variety of special powers, and they were able to pass them on to their offspring. What these beings did with their special powers had to do with their capacity to know right from wrong and good from bad. The decisions of these organisms had shaped and affected their societies as numerous civilizations developed over the centuries.

PART 1

CHAPTER 1

Zorax's Adventure Begins

Each of the twenty-six galaxies in the universe had its own name, and each started with a different letter of the alphabet. It was custom that the names of inhabitants of each galaxy began with the same letter as their galaxy's name. This made it easy to recognize their kind—and those from other galaxies. No one ever was confused as to another's origins or found it unsafe, because it was only used as an organized system to keep government records and the history of each world.

The inhabitants who lived in these different galaxies were what would be typically called aliens because they had their own specific physical characteristics. They did not resemble all the normal traits of earth humans. Nevertheless, they were living beings with families and houses and cars and jobs—if where they lived was a well-developed nation or society. They were young and old and female and male. They all went through the process of finding their place in the Azzon world. They all had to make choices about who they wanted to be and the path they wanted to follow. Some chose wisely, but some did not.

It was a late evening, a couple centuries after the extraordinary power surge incident. Millions of creatures had been changed in the way they lived their lives and what they chose to do. A legendary hero and his fearless friends had taken a stand in their own galaxy unit and ended up restoring peace, unity, and balance to the universe.

It was the beginning of the International Planetary Civilization Development era (IPCD). There was significant trading between different worlds around the universe and great amounts of imports and exports of goods and resources. After building spaceships and other extraterrestrial traveling machines, various nations were able to communicate and negotiate. Individual leaders from nearby planets later agreed to meet up and converse about ideas on a good government system that would benefit the whole group of neighboring planets.

After all the officials had agreed, a law was passed called the *Galaxy Unit Act* in 1888 Azzon time, which stated that an individual was to rule as king or queen over several worlds, and that they would obtain the majority power of making decisions about what was best for their people. However, the citizens under that chief's rule would still have the power to vote against certain actions made by the sovereign and the opportunity to elect for whom they would like to have in control of their kingdom. In case of a sudden need for a replacement of the current leader, there was always an assistant king or queen who was properly trained to take the role of the previous royal official and continue in his or her footsteps. Usually, that runner-up acted as an assistant to the present ruler and helped with the decisions that the ruler was making and tips for what and how to do things in difficult times of an economy's struggle.

It was a calm, relaxing evening in the city of Zorgatopolis on the planet Zorga. This rapidly developing society had skyscrapers, factories, and was the center of all big businesses. Hover jets and cars roared past the city landmarks in the ultimate speed of light, zooming by like NASCAR racers in midair in different directions. The tiny red and yellow stars were hidden behind the thick purple skies as fractions of light were let loose through small cracks in the heavy clouds.

As high-tech as this section of this world may have seemed, it was still developing; seventy-five percent of the transportation vehicles were still operating on the ground. Only aliens in the upper class or a little above average standard in economic or social positions could ride the public off-ground transportation or afford personal hover cars.

Thousands of aliens strolled around the busy and chaotic cities into the peaceful neighborhoods of the suburbs where many people went about their business completing daily tasks. Adults worked in and out of homes, children went to school and played in the grassy fields, and the population of the city continued to grow rapidly as fast as the technology, which was a significant period during the reign of the Zemus Kingdom.

One of these common civilians was a teenage alien strolling down the brick pedestrian pathway in his neighborhood. Zorax Zoomster had light green skin and a football-shaped head, on top of which was a small antenna. As part of the Zorgalian species, he could breathe and withstand the air pressure and temperature of open space without the shelter of a spaceship or an astronaut suit. For the most part, his body was similar to humans. He was around one and a half Zuzu berry trees tall, had light brown eyes, and wore an orange sleeveless T-shirt made of smooth wild-creature skin, dark blue silk pants, and shiny red shoes made from a rich rubber material that grew beneath the ground in his hometown. His age averaged around two thousand Zellonians (or sixteen human years old).

Looking at the grocery list in his hand, he wondered if he was forgetting anything. He rubbed his fingers across the top of his head and squinted as he reread the foods and necessities that he had already jotted down. Before he could think any harder, he sensed a sudden danger or uneasiness that was nearby disturbing the peace. Then he heard random screams of panic and distress coming from all around the block. He immediately looked up in curiosity as his heart made a quick jump. People swerved their cars sideways on the street as if they were heading for the edge of a cliff and busted through the doors and looked up in shock. Mothers, who were once walking and playing with their children, grabbed their hands and began running for their lives. Families ran out of their homes into their yards and joined the others who watched the sky with extremely worried expressions. There was so much chaos that numerous collisions occurred on the streets because so many people were trying to escape the disaster that was coming from the sky. Huge amounts of Zorgalians fled on foot away from what seemed to be the center of the city. Stampedes started to form and entered other busy streets of traffic because the people in the crowds could not escape from the ridiculous traffic jam on the highways and intersections. The aliens hopped over cars and—if they were really daring and desperate—ran in front of moving vehicles.

Zorax could see the gigantic blobs of townspeople rushing toward him like herds of buffalo. As they advanced, he was absolutely frightened as his eyes widened and he slowly stepped back. Surprisingly, when the rushing frenzy did arrive at the spot where he was standing, they ran around him and continued to dash down the pathway for their lives. Most of the aliens in the uncivilized group stared or glanced at the one person who was still calm and unhesitant. As they passed him, they yelled "Kid, get outta the way!" and "What are you doing? Run for your life while you still can!"

Although they didn't run into him completely, he was nudged and shoved aggressively and eventually knocked brutally to the ground. Immediately, he put his hands over his head as if he were being stopped by the police and rolled on his side as he heard the wild movement of feet stomping past him without a care that he was on the floor. As he got up after the last couple of inhabitants shot by in the group, he patted his chest lightly as he began to cough uncontrollably, inhaling the dust that had been brought up by the obnoxious movement.

In a brief moment, he got to his feet and examined the behavior of his surroundings again. Dusting off his shirt and pants, he could see increasingly Zorgalians rushing in large groups away from the city, which seemed to becoming larger by the second. The various noises that echoed from the highly populated area sounded louder into the neighborhoods of the suburban territories.

Zorax, in the middle of the dirt road, glanced behind him when a band of spontaneous sirens went off with outrageous flashing lights of yellow and green rotating in the air. Just in time, he was able to think fast and hop back onto the pedestrian pathway before getting run over by a police squadron on jet bikes. Jet bikes were similar to the structure of a motorcycle, except that they were made of titanium, hovered over ground, and accelerated to hundreds of miles per hour in under thirty-seconds. There were three of them zooming down through the middle of the town in amazing speeds, covering the whole place in thick dust all again as it raised into the air and vanished later on. Zorax overheard them saying, "Come on, let's go, let's move, those people are in danger down there! Can't this lousy thing go any faster?"

Zorax still had no clue about what was going on, but he kept hearing his neighbors shouting, "This is the end! Our day of doom has finally come!" and "That thing will wipe us all out when it hits the ground!" and "We have to get off of this planet quickly!"

Finally, everything made sense when the confused teen looked up and saw an enormous and lethal meteorite plummeting straight for his home planet—even worse, directly at his hometown. In about four to five minutes, if something didn't change its course, the meteorite would turn the planet into fragments and dust and everyone on it would be instantly erased from existence. Zorax had that something. Zorax was among those exposed to the extraordinary mist of the gems released by Dr. Zillozongo. His specific power was telekinesis, which was the one of the most common abilities passed down from the history of his ancestors.

"What's the matter with ya, Zorax? Are ya crazy? Hurry up and get inside and take cover before it's too late!"

The young Zorgalian jolted back and put his hand up in response. "Uh . . . that's okay, Mr. Zallobee. I'm fine. Matter of fact, I'll think I'll take a look for myself and check out what's going on down there. Don't worry. I won't be long!" He started to run toward the disordered commotion in the hectic streets up ahead.

"What! Have you lost your mind? You'll get killed if you go down there!" Mr. Zallobee cautioned.

"Sorry, but we're all gonna die anyway the way I see it in the end. I'm afraid you can't stop me."

"That boy never listens. He's always looking for trouble." Mr. Zallobee shook his head and went back through the door in his hut across the pathway from Zorax's house.

He went farther south of Zorgatoplis, trying to avoid running into the hundreds of panicking pedestrians dodging them as if raging bullets were being fired at him. Getting closer to the havoc of the intersections, he could see traffic backed up for miles. The level of intensity increased when the irritating alarms of the police rang louder and the furious drivers honked more aggressively; thousands of people who were in their vehicles could not get out and were trapped in a bumper-to-bumper situation.

Leaping over the roofs of cars and trucks, he made his way to a humongous bridge that arched over the expressway. Some dazed folks were just watching the final horror. Spotting a truck in the middle of the road, its driver in distress and surrounded by tiny cars, he finally found his chance to complete his brave and bold action. When Zorax climbed the long ladder at the back of the massive mover, the driver watched the violating stranger. As if he already had enough issues, the driver stormed out of the front seat and followed him to the rear.

Zorax positioned himself with a firm stance and focused on the danger. When he looked down, an oversized man was screaming at the top of his lungs with a very hoarse voice, threatening to come up.

"Just what exactly do you think you're doing up there? Don't you see that thing coming for us all? Are ya trying to get a better look or something? Get down here before I get really angry! You better not make me come up there, ya little hooligan. Do you hear me?"

Ignoring the commands of the outraged adult, he turned back to the sky, which seemed to be getting darker, and stretched his hands into the air as the mighty meteorite demolished small transportation ships in the air with its extremely powerful and intimidating size. The brutal impact left specks of metal after the explosions. His small antenna glowing a bright red, Zorax put his hands up toward the plunging space rock and—just as it seemed that destruction was unavoidable and as the last horrific cries and screams broke out—the meteorite abruptly paused and spun backward with the correct rotations of his hands, moving as fast away from the planet's atmosphere as it had come.

In a few minutes, it was gone, swallowed up by outer space and was nowhere to be seen. Zorax's remarkable rescue had saved the planet from an apocalypse. People stood and sat in awe for a few seconds and then immediately broke out into joy and relief. Before he knew it, drivers climbed out of their cars to cheer and clap for Zorax. From all over the city, the rumor spread like wildfire of his heroic action. Surprisingly, even the truck driver joined and admired the hero with great applause.

"Way to go!" they shouted. Other aliens ran onto the bridge to shake Zorax's hand and cheered. "Thank you! You saved us!"

In less than a minute, more people were on the bridge than cars and police. Nearby city officials had to enter swiftly before things got out of line and made sure traffic ran smoothly and Zorax made it out okay. Two construction workers picked up the highly honored adolescent and put him on their shoulders, walking off the bridge, while people rejoiced and jumped all about in gratefulness. News reporters barged their way through the crazy crowd to take pictures of the flattered teen because there was too much tumult to get an interview.

By the time, the citizens had finished thanking Zorax, and the outstanding level of energy wore down, it was getting late and he still had to go to the market. Like before, many Zorgalians of all ages ran up to him with the most positive things to say. As he walked into the mini mart, he saw himself on a television with the local news in the uproar of the most memorable event of the year. He didn't quite notice, but many customers who seemed very occupied making their way through the narrow aisles stopped in their tracks in amazement that the hero that saved their lives was right there in the store. Little whispers broke out between various shoppers; one employee who was stacking goods on a shelf immediately stopped what he was doing and ran into the back of the store.

Too busy gathering supplies and goods in his basket to notice the enthusiastic costumers around him, Zorax made his way to the check-out station where a tall green-skinned woman with short blue hair and brown eyes walked up to him with a big smile and introduced herself.

"Hi, I'm Zola Zekingstein. Nice to meet you!"

"Hi? Zorax Zoomster, same to you," he said, noticing that something was up and that no person would offer to be that pleasant just plainly like that.

"Can I help you with anything today?"

"I—"

"Never mind that. You've done such a good job today for our nation that you can have anything you want here and as much of anything as you want and for free! How's that sound?"

"Really? Cause I was just gonna come check out my items and I wouldn't feel right if I just walked right out without—"

"Nonsense, my boy, now do hurry. Our store does close soon, you know?"

"Okay, miss. Thanks." Zorax was so delighted that he bought a little more than he had originally gone in for.

After the unexpected act of kindness, he arrived home at around the middle of the second dark hour—or eight thirty—with his favorite snack combo, brain juice boxes and moon pies. He was tired and hungry, but he felt good. It was the perfect thing to end his day with a refreshing can of sweet mixed berry and animal blood flavored juice and a slice of creamy and fluffy pastry that could be compared to the taste of eggnog mixed with marshmallow. Even though this meal may have not been the healthiest, the hardworking teen decided he deserved it and gave in to the sugary temptation.

After a good night's sleep, Zorax went outside to play with his dog Vanilla. Vanilla was, of course, the color of vanilla. He was medium sized, with an antenna on his head like Zorax's and had floppy ears. He had a small shiny black nose and wore a red collar that stood out brightly against his light fur. On the other hand, since Vanilla wasn't a regular canine, he was able to walk on two legs or four perfectly fine and his special lungs allowed him to be able to breathe in space temporarily. He could also speak the native Zorgalian language and communicate well with other aliens. Vanilla was not Zorgalian, but of an alien canine race called Vanderian-Carnians, who had an unusual system where the males were named with the letter "v" and females by "c." In other words, he was not at all any ordinary pet—probably more of a friend who was part of the family.

A small blue moon called Zelspar glowed in the purple sky, shining over the city and suburbs of Zorgatapolis. Zorga only had one moon, and because it had no sun, Zelspar was its only source of light. There were twenty-six hours in a day on Zorga. The environment on Zorga was a natural rocky and dirt terrain with many tall and bushy trees that grew up to twelve feet tall. For the most part, the weather was calm with damp spring air and cool winds. The buildings and houses were constructed of a hard smooth blue and grayish stone called Zalpayhte, commonly found underground in urban areas; it was strong enough to withstand minor hurricanes or twisters.

Zorax's house was a two-flat townhome, painted in an attractive sky blue with tall white pillars that supported the foundation. The lawn was covered in neatly trimmed grass that was divided by a pathway made of polished Zalpayhte. Young teenage aliens were supported financially by their parents or other elderly relatives until they were able to get a job.

Just as Zorax tossed the Frisbee toward Vanilla, there was a loud whirring above him. This was no meteorite. Before he could even figure out what the noise was, the sky was suddenly filled with menacing, vast gray and black round spaceships. Beams of light shot from a turret on top of the ships toward the planet and one of those beams flashed on Vanilla. Zorax had no time to save his beloved Vanilla who was sucked up into the light like dust into a vacuum cleaner and he instantly vanished. The terrified Zorgalian tried to chase the spaceship, but the dirt road a few feet away from his yard began heaving around him, chunks of pavement flying around his head, some of them smashing into his chest. Struggling through the unforeseen disaster, Zorax used some handy psychic energy to escape the destruction and then immediately dashed to his backyard where he parked his vehicle and jumped into his dark red ZUV he had gotten as a birthday present a couple years earlier. He flew it over to his friend Zork's house, a couple blocks north from the city. Since average space cars were about as fast as a small jet plane, Zorax arrived at Zork's house in no time flat.

Out of breath, he ran to Zork's household and told him the story of the beam of light and the disappearance of Vanilla. He was desperate to get his dog back and begged Zork to help.

"Whoa, whoa, whoa, slow down. So you were playing Frisbee and then what happened?"

"And then these random wild ships came tearing through my neighborhood and one of them shot down this tractor beam thing and—"

"We're about to crash!" Zork yelled.

"Hang on!" screamed Zorax.

The alien companions screamed as their car shut down and began to be pulled diagonally by a strong gravitational force. They fell out of their seats and held hands tightly as the material and parts of the car begun to fly off and the acceleration of the controlled vehicle was increasing uncontrollably rapid. Before they knew it, half of the automobile was on fire, and then they blacked out!

*   *   *

Fifteen minutes later, they woke to find themselves on Zepula. The planet's surface and atmosphere were freezing with slippery ice and piles of snow. Just as they thought they might freeze to death, a kind, young sensei appeared. Noticing that they were outsiders and needed help desperately, he took them to a warm, cozy hut, and handed them cups of warm creamy moon milk.

The sensei, Zemo, possessed the mystical power of ice. Zemo was slightly tall with light brown skin and hazel eyes. His head contained bright brown shiny hair with a single antenna, and he wore a blue and white puffy overcoat with black buttons that ran down the middle. It was part of the Zepulian culture to help strangers in need. He asked them where they were coming from and where they had been planning on going.

"Coming from Zorga, going to Zemustopeia," Zorax replied.

"Oh—what are you planning to do there?" Zemo inquired.

"To retrieve my dog Vanilla back from that malicious Zemus; we suspect he has him," said Zorax.

"King Zemus? He is the most powerful person in the galaxy unit!" Zemo exclaimed.

"Come on! You've gotta be bluffing a little, right?" Zork said. "We survived a ship crash—I'm pretty sure we can take on Zemus's forces."

"Speaking of the crash . . . do you know how we survived? Shouldn't we have been dead from the impact or at least pretty banged up from it?" questioned Zempunella.

"That's easy. If you didn't know already, in this part of town, the snowy fields are surprisingly made of extra fluff that can stop anything from hitting the ground too hard. That explains why you weren't hurt after you were thrown from your ship."

"Basically we pretty much got lucky," Zorax said.

"Yep," said Zemo. "And now that I think of it—that does make sense why most of the playgrounds are built there."

"I can live with that," Zork said.

"Now that we realize we're not as tough as we thought, we're back to square one. Is there really any hope for us?" Zempunella sought for an answer.

"What should I do?" Zorax asked rethinking his overconfident and slightly unrealistic strategy.

"You can stay and train with me in my dojo. I am a brother of three; you can practice with them for the battle with the king."

Meeting Zemo almost made up for the crash, Zorax thought, as he and his friends walked to the hotel where he would stay the night and begin practicing with Zemo in the morning.

The next day, while he practiced, Zempunella and Zork would prepare in other ways for the fight to reclaim Vanilla.

The next morning, Zorax went from his hotel room across the street to the dojo were Zemo trained. The first lesson was to use his powers to change the elements. This training of mystical powers and abilities by alien beings was known as Mushi. Zemo placed a cup of boiling water in front of Zorax. Steam from the water rose into the air and eventually disappeared.

"Now, Zorax," Zemo said. "I want you to concentrate and make this water freeze."

Zorax focused as hard as he could, squinting his eyes and trying to make the water stop steaming, but nothing happened. He tried again, straining so hard he began to sweat. "I can't do this," he said.

"It's okay—just relax," Zemo said.

Zorax tried one more time. He took a deep breath and focused hard and slowly. His antenna began to glow faintly blue and out the end of it, a tiny blizzard of snowflakes fell right into the cup of hot water. In a few seconds, it turned to ice. Zorax grinned, amazed at his newfound ability. "Thank you!" he said. "That's incredible!"

"Excellent. Nice work. You see, all you need to do is keep your focus on what you need to accomplish and eventually it will come. Not only in training but in everything you do in life."

"I'll try to remember that," Zorax responded humbly.

Zemo informed Zorax that his antennae color reflected a certain color light, and color is determined by the power that is currently being used.

ZORAX'S POWERS	ANTENNAE COLORS
TELEKINESIS	RED
FREEZING/ICE	LIGHT BLUE
WATER	DARK BLUE
FIRE	ORANGE

After days of challenging and helpful practice, the travel team had to go to the next planet. While Zorax was training, Zempunella and Zork had bought a used space car which was surprisingly cheap. The exploratory colleagues got into the space car and blasted off into the open area again. They waved good-bye to Zemo and headed to the third planet of the galaxy unit known as Zorgatto. They checked the map for the next pit stop. There was a fuel station a couple miles west, on Milky Way Street. Zempunella, reading the map saw this: ***Danger: Be cautious.*** The area was obviously an upcoming danger zone.

Zork was on the lookout, but he could not see anything with his binoculars. Not too long after, the group witnessed a meteor shower later. Trying to stop the meteors with his telekinesis or maneuver around them, Zorax attempted, but there were too many it would be impossible. He made himself attentive like he had recently learned and his antennae shined to a shade of azure; with a spontaneous flash of light in the blink of an eye, all the meteors were instantly frozen.

"Wow!" said Zempunella. "How'd you do that?"

"That was awesome!" said Zork.

"Thanks," said Zorax. "It was a little something I picked up with Zemo's teaching back on Zepula."

"It's a good thing you did or else we would have been taken out for good," Zork said.

"You can say that again," Zempunella said. "All right, maybe we can find a main pathway or something if we keep on this track."

"Good idea. I'll be on the lookout!" replied Zorax.

Relieved at their escape, the three Zorgalians saw a sign toward the galactic express, which they decided to take so they could get to their destination quicker. On the expressway, there were millions of space cars and ships at furious speeds in every direction possible. As Zorax manipulated his own car into a lane, there was a loud siren from behind.

"Ugh . . . what's the matter with these people? Don't they know how to fly properly?" Zorax avoided numerous collisions from the wild strangers that passed by.

"Not to pick sides or anything, but maybe they're running from that loud noise," Zork said.

"What is that? It's getting louder as we speak." Zempunella glued her face to the window.

Not too long after that, the curious group found out that it was the police chasing a getaway space wagon jam-packed with muggers. The traffic caused by this incident was unbelievably dreadful; the gang was stuck in their car for five long hours. When they finally got to the fuel post, the police were staked out around it; the depraved offenders had taken the cashier hostage and were snatching wads of cash from the register.

"Finally we're here," Zorax said. "This traffic is insane. How much slower could we possibly go?"

"I think I might know why?" Zork said. "Aren't those the same police officers we saw earlier on the rampage for those crooks!"

"Wait a second you're right! Oh no you don't think that there's a—" Zorax conjectured.

"There's only one way to find out," Zempunella said, exiting the ship.

"Wait! Zempunella where are you—"

Zorax's younger sister approached the small store, where she walked by numerous police ships with the officials standing beside them armed with guns. They watched as she boldly prepared to enter the crime scene. One of them stopped her before she could go any further.

"Missy, just what do you think you're doing?"

"What does it look like? I'm obviously about to save the day," she said.

"That's cute. I appreciate the bravery, little girl, but this is no place for you right now. How about you run along from wherever you came from and I will take care of everything?"

"Really, like that half-eaten box of moon pies in the passenger seat of your ship?"

"Listen, this is the last time I'm going to say this, kid! Get out of here right now before you get yourself into trouble!"

"Whatever you say." Zempunella walked away slowly until the authorities took their eyes off her—and then she hid behind one of the fuel dispensers.

Zempunella decided to use her own special powers to do some good. Her antennae flickered silver and her whole body turned invisible. She sneaked back through the doors, and went up behind the burglars.

"Whoa! Did you see that?" one of the men said.

"What?"

"The doors? I could've sworn I just saw them swing open for a second! You don't think these criminals are ghosts do you? Or maybe this place is haunted?"

"Would you stop being so ridiculous? It was probably just the wind. I'm sure of it. Now be quiet and pass me another moon pie. I'm starving."

The store was filled with long shelves that stacked snacks, candy, and sports drinks. Two cashiers on their knees with their hands in the air were begging for their lives. One of the bandits continued to empty bundles of money into a large garbage bag while the other had a gun pointed at the heads of the captives.

"Please! Just let us go! We promise we won't stop you or call the police!"

"We'll do whatever you guys want us to. Just please don't fire!"

The two hostages seemed to be a married couple. Zempunella knew she had to act quickly knowing that they would die from a heart attack before even possibly getting shot.

"Silence, you incompetent fools! Can't you see that they are already here?"

"For people who own this store for a living . . . you're not very observant to say the least. Don't worry; we still need you to make our clean getaway. When they see that we have you with us, they'll refuse to take further action to try to stop us.

"You said it, Zimmy. This plan couldn't have worked out any more perfectly."

"I wouldn't be so sure. However, I admire your optimism," Zempunella found humor with a minor giggle.

"What! Who said that? Show yourself! Now!"

"Come out from wherever you're hiding right now or one of these lovely workers goes bye-bye for the day!"

"Are you really sure you wanna do that? From the looks of it, you're already in enough trouble as it is. Do you really wanna add more to your plate of problems?"

"Err! Quit hiding!" The gunmen began shooting up the store, knocking over items on shelves, and shattering the glass windows and doors.

"Wow. Somebody has a bad temper," said Zempunella. "All right, as much fun as this is, I think it's time to finish this—don't you think?"

"You're right!" The felon looked ready to shoot one of the employees.

She took a rope that she had found in the trash behind the building, and tied up the two bandits before they could commit any harm. The cashiers stood in disbelief. She immediately snatched the gun from their hands and kicked

it across the floor—along with the bag of money
gave back to the rescued citizens.

"I can't move!"

"Good, that's how it should be! Looks like th
back to normal, huh?" she remarked revealing herse

"What! I don't believe it! We got beat by
But . . . that's not even possible!"

The couple got to their feet and ran up to Zem
"Wow, you were amazing! I've never seen such bra
such a young one before!" the women said.

"Yes, I absolutely agree! That was truly somethi
don't happen to work for the police force, do you?"

"No, sir," Zempunella said. "Just an ordinary g

"For an ordinary girl, you sure did more than th
cops out there. What were they doing? Were they
for something else to happen?"

"Now, sweetheart, there must be something we
for you now."

"Not really . . . the only reason I'm here is bec
friends and I needed some fuel and . . ."

"Say no more! It's free! And if you even nee
snacks for the trip, feel free to take whatever yo
Please! It's the least we can do!" the woman said.

"If you insist. Thanks."

"No, thank you!"

Suddenly, a trio of cops busted through the do

"Is everything okay, folks? I thought we told y
home, little girl!"

"Excuse me, officer, but thanks to this little g
still alive no thanks to you!"

"This is awkward . . . we didn't expect that."

"Yeah, but good job anyway. You really impr
today," Zempunella said as she walked out of the s
a couple items in her hand.

dn't pay for those! Are you really just gonna sit
there someone steal something from your store like
that main officer yelled.

ttle too late for that catchphrase, don't ya think?"
the said with her hands on her hips.

lly, the cops arrested the lawbreakers. After the
rove refilled their fuel tank, they continued their
exp

e wondering what took you so long. We started
to d. Did you really defeat those guys without any
trorax asked unable to conceive it.

!"

y really gave us this food for free along with
thrk added.

n guys really didn't think those police officers
wo something now, did you?"

she does have a point," Zork said.

CHAPTER 2

Prison Pals

Vanilla's spaceship dungeon wasn't the most sanitary place to be in—and it did not contain the best odor either. The vessel contained many of Zemus's ruthless guards who continuously patrolled the area. Apparently, the tractor beam that had caught Vanilla was a temporary accident that was made by a new troop of little experience who was flying the craft at the time. When the spacecraft landed on Zemustopeia, Vanilla was forced into a claustrophobic prison at the vile villain's mansion.

King Zemus was a millionaire, who had his own planet. His money had been received illegally from extra taxes levied upon innocent people all over the galaxy unit. Everyone hated and feared the corrupt dictator, but they would never dare to rebel or protest against his orders. They knew the drastic consequences that would immediately follow if they did so.

To keep his grand scheme a secret, he made sure that none of the other rulers knew who were in charge of the outer galaxy units. If the royal council ever found out, he would have come across serious penalties. Originally, Zemus wasn't wicked. He was born into a poor family, but he grew

"Wow, it actually worked! We make a relatively good team."

"Yep," Vanilla exclaimed. "Let's get outta here!"

They dashed down the dark corridors, which had a few rows of tiny white bulbs of light at the tops of the walls. When they peeked around the corner, they saw three guards by a larger exit that led out of the detention sector of the ship.

"Great. What are we gonna do now?" Zella said.

"Stand by," Vanilla whispered. "I have an idea. Just follow my lead with whatever you can do."

"I hope you know what you're doing," Zella said.

"I hope you do too because if I don't, then we're both going down," Vanilla remarked partially joking and caveat.

Vanilla's antennae steadily warped to purple and, because he could shape shift, he was able to transform himself into a replica of one of the guards. He could walk past the other security troops without being recognized.

"Whoa!" Zella observed rubbing her eyes to confirm that her sight wasn't deceiving her.

"I know—cool, right?"

Vanilla waltzed away toward the danger ahead. He approached the squad of suspicious militaries. They watched him as he advanced in their direction.

"Trooper, you're not supposed to be back there and especially not by yourself. Where is the rest of your patrol crew? You should know the new rule by now, yes?"

Vanilla walked with swagger until he was directly in front of them, throwing back the same amount of intimidation that they gave him.

The captain and his colleagues grew impatient as they closed in on him.

"Rookie, don't you hear the general talking to you?"

"Just who do you think you are?"

Daringly, Vanilla transformed into his normal form right before their eyes. They rubbed their eyes in disbelief much like Zella beforehand.

"What the—" the captain yelled, directing his gun at Vanilla. "What the heck are you?"

"Slick!" Vanilla laughed, looking down with a devious smirk.

Zella jumped out from behind and released raging ice rays from her fingertips with an unusual verbal saying that froze the confused aliens before they had time to react.

"Nice one," Vanilla cried. "I knew you would catch on eventually about when to come in!"

"Eh, I was just getting tired of watching you, but you were good out there."

"Let's keep moving," Vanilla advised with a sense of humor.

He and Zella found their selves on the main floor of the mansion after climbing a few flights of stairs, which seemed to be endless. Although, it was owned by such an uncivilized being it was unbelievably attractive with golden doors, silver vases, crystal chandeliers, and bronze elevators. The ground was made of rich-colored stone tiles that were layered with red and gold velvet carpets that stretched a couple yards throughout the home. The walls were decorated with portraits of Zemus. Ice sculptures of him were built inside and out of the kingdom, complemented by spring fountains that were constructed around the perimeter. The problem was that the manor was so immense it was impossible to find their way out.

Zella accidentally leaned on a vase and a red button popped up.

"I wonder what this does,"

"Wait. No don't—"

But it was too late—she pressed it, the floor opened up beneath them, and without warning they fell through a long six foot vent-like tunnel onto a huge pile of dirty laundry. Above them, the hole through which they had fallen closed back up.

"-Press that!" Vanilla pulled fabric from his mouth.

"Sorry," Zella said, trying to break free out of the colossal clump of clothes. "Where are we now?"

"I don't know, but please don't press any more buttons." Vanilla got to his feet, rubbing his head.

After exploring the room, they realized they were in a clandestine lab filled with papers and books that had preposterous ideas and plans for the most destructive machines imaginable. As they were skimming over the complicated scientifically drawn diagrams, they heard a noise. King Zemus and five Zorogon sentinels came through the main entrance toward a spaceship that sat in a nearby garage area.

Zemus obtained most of the traits of the Zemustopeian raise but since his mother was from another galaxy, he did not resemble the citizens on the planet too much. He had bright yellow skin, a shiny set of silver teeth, and razor sharp claws. His golden crown was encrusted with jewels; on his balloon-shaped head, one antenna draped down like a flower without water on his head. A long red velvet gown covered his body from his shoulders to his feet with white fluffy cotton at the bottom. His ears looked like little tube holes and his nose was black.

"Shhh, get behind those boxes. Hurry!"

The ship that he possessed was one of strongest and fastest in the galaxy unit known as the ZX6. Apparently, Zemus was going to a news broadcast building to make an announcement about the economy. As the spacecraft took off, Vanilla and Zella came out from hiding.

"Where do you think he's going?" Zella asked.

"I don't know, but we're gonna find out," Vanilla said. "Come on! At least we can get out this way too!"

The adventurous pals jumped into a small orange UFO and followed him closely.

"You are a good flyer, right?" Zella concerned.

"I've flown a couple times. But nothing as small as this thing . . . we should be okay."

"All right, I hope you're right. Anyway I have a question."

"What is it?"

"No offense but . . . aren't you from one of the farthest galaxies from here?"

"Yeah . . . Is that a problem?"

"No, not at all, but I heard that your race was used as . . . um . . ."

"Pets?"

"I'm sorry. I didn't wanna say it in a way that was offensive. Maybe we should just talk about something else."

"No, relax! It's cool. Yes, it's true. My race was known as wild before, but the charmed gas affected the current dwellers on my home planet, Vandora. Oddly enough, my people did not only receive powers, but they were changed from their wild behavior and became civilized beings. After that remarkable phase, they started to interact with others from other planets and slowly developed their own nations . . . and that's essentially what happened."

"Okay, but that still doesn't explain how you are able to talk, speak the common language in this galaxy, make it all the way over here, and if you had a better mind of your own how were you kept as a pet?" Zella rambled on with endless thoughts.

"Whoa, whoa, whoa, slow down! Maybe I wasn't too clear about my life, but just take it easy with the questions. This isn't an interview . . . you're not gonna give up, are you?"

"Nope," Zella teased.

"What if I told you that I was born before the distribution of the diamond gas?"

"That's not possible! It happened a long time ago!"

"Yeah, well the truth is I've been alive for that long."

"Really? You can't die of old age?"

"No, I can . . . the thing is that it takes a long time for my race to age . . . a really, really long time as you can see. Certainly, I'm gonna be around for a long time . . . if I . . . don't get myself into too much danger."

"No kidding . . . that's amazing!"

"Yeah . . . but that's kind of not all of it. Before I went into my transformation stage, I was adopted by my friend Zorax's ancestors and passed down the generation of his family. They bought me at a store that these outsiders came and put my people in. I was the one of few who was somewhat tame so they chose us to sell. I was eventually Zorax's present before he was born. His progenitors were on a reunion trip with some of their friends from a close planet to ours and came to mine to visit. When I was with them on Zorga, the crazy thing happened with the powers and you know the rest."

"Wow, that's a lot," Zella said in astonishment.

"Yep, it was weird at first, but we got used to it after a while. It was worth it. Zorax and the others back at home are awesome. Now it's time for me to ask you something."

"All right, fair enough . . . go ahead."

"You know back there when we ambushed those guards?"

"Yeah . . . what about it?"

"I've never seen anyone with your ability."

"You might not know it, but the ability to use ice is fairly common in the Zepulian population. Even my neighbor Zemo is a grand master at it."

"I don't mean that. Sorry, I meant that weird saying while you were doing it."

"Oh, those are just words I use to activate my powers."

"Really? I didn't understand a thing you said."

"That's because they're from an ancient Zepulian language from before the whole galaxy started speaking one language. Those prehistoric sayings can be translated into words and terms in our current language. I have the book that does that stuff at home."

"Wow, you mean to tell me that you have to remember a different saying for every different move you do?"

"Not exactly. Some sayings I can use for more than one thing and I'm still learning this new technique which is called Verbal Mushi. I just picked it up recently. Besides I still have to concentrate really hard . . . it's not like I can just say whatever and it will happen . . . it's just what was passed onto me."

"Interesting, I still think I'd prefer without the talking to do something. When you're strong enough, you'll be able to totally equipped much do anything you want, right?"

"I guess so, but that won't be for a long while," Zella said.

"I think he's going inside that building," Vanilla said.

"Seems like it. I wonder what he's planning to do there."

"There's only one way to find out."

The monarch parked in a garage under the tremendous communication tower. The spying scouts had to park a good distance away because they did not want Zemus to identify his stolen vehicle.

As the villain entered the building, he went to a large room on the fifth floor and busted through the doors. Many of the workers in the office immediately stood up and bowed to their royal ruler.

"Get back to work!" Zemus screamed, barging through to the camera set up.

In a blue fluffy velvet chair, he had his employees running around doing paperwork, physical labor, and whatever else he demanded.

The two breakout buddies hid behind a table of refreshments after sneaking into the message room. The workers were way too occupied to notice their presence.

"I wonder what scam this scum is trying to run now!" said Vanilla.

"Hurry. Get under the table! Zemus's goons are coming over!" Zella whispered.

The barbaric Zorogons rushed over to the snack table, knocking away or trampling any of the workers that were in their way. As they fought over the moon pies and crumble cakes, chunks and crumbs flew from their loud mouths as they chugged zogo berry smoothies and cans of moon milk. The table was shook rambunctiously as if an earthquake was occurring as the unmannerly minions released heavy belches and burps with repulsive stenches.

"Hungry much?" said Zella, covering her nose.

"Shhh . . . wait! I think that crook is just about getting ready to start!" Vanilla lifted the tablecloth and peeked past the bulky hairy legs of the starving Zorogons.

"Hurry it up, will ya?" Zemus said. "I don't have all day to watch you have no life!"

"Forgive me, Your Majesty. You're on in three, two, one."

"Good evening, citizens of the galaxy unit. I have noticed that the tax payments have dropped in the past months quite drastically, and I would love for you ignorant and unreliable creatures to meet the required expectations for once. If you fail to please me in the upcoming weeks, I will without a doubt or second thought, gladly conjure up another severe consequence due to your constant and stubborn rebellion. Believe me—it will be worse than the one last week. Since you refuse to meet my standards at paying the required price, I am going to triple taxes on everything, starting on galactic fuel for space crafts. Thank you!"

Shocked by the cruelty of monarchism in their society, Vanilla and Zella shared numerous glances in reaction to what they just witnessed. As King Zemus made way out of the edifice and embarked his high-tech traveler, zooming off at light speed.

"We need to stop him!" Zella darted with Vanilla toward the ship.

"We will!" Vanilla flew as fast as he could toward the Zemustopeia town square where Zemus was.

CHAPTER 3

Spaceship Battle

King Zemus was preparing the process to halt his ship and retrieve some groceries at no cost when a bold space car from behind fired two spontaneous missiles that damaged the side of his luxurious shuttle. Ferocious flames erupted with foggy puffs of smoke as the ZX6 wobbled in a slightly unstable condition. He and the Zorogons fell to the floor as the alarm warning rang obnoxiously; they slowly got up to their feet, recovering from the huge hit.

"What was that?" Zemus asked his temper resurrected in no time flat.

"Yeah, that hurt," the pilot added, rubbing his head from where he made brutal interaction with the dashboard.

"It looks like we have a rebellion of some sort, sir," the captain reported.

"I should've known to expect poorly thought out attempts from unwise demonstrators in times like these to try to stop me in my tracks. Destroy them! Make sure they do not escape! I want you to demolish their pathetic ship to smithereens with them inside!"

"As you wish, Your Highness. You heard the boss, troopers, let's move out!"

Zemus's five guards disappeared from his presence in separate war crafts attached to his larger one to complete their given task of defense while he called for assistance from his home base to pick him up.

The maneuvering minions emitted highly concentrated gunfire from their ammunition blasters at Vanilla and Zella's spacecraft, but the two companions were too quick for them and easily dodged the incoming shots.

After the success of incredible navigation in avoiding their enemies' assaults, the adroit acquaintances saved up enough time to launch another pair of rockets. Each made direct contact and obliterated a battle craft.

"Excellent! We have two ships down and three more to go!" Zella shouted with ebullient excitement.

"Eh, the way I see it now . . . piece of cake!" Vanilla said.

"Come on guys, hang in there!" the Zorogon captain said. "Are we honestly gonna let these amateurs beat us?"

The next battleship caught the heroes by surprise when it ejected an electrical ray laser and knocked off their rearview mirror. Zella took action from curiosity of a blue button and a cannon folded out from the bottom of the UFO fighter releasing an enormous yellow beam that vaporized two more soaring opponents.

"Wow! That's was amazing! I didn't even know we had that feature!" said Zella more than satisfied with what her audacious interest brought.

"Let's not get too carried away," Vanilla alerted. "This isn't over yet."

"Those pitiful soldiers!" the general said. "After all these years of training, they were taken down so simply by some rookies! How disgraceful! I guess it's up to me to teach these twerps a lesson on what happens to pests like them who dare challenge the wrath of Zemus's army force!"

The chief's module was exceedingly swift and doubled the speed of the normal ones from before. As lasers and missiles were continuously fired, many missed and destroyed local stores, houses, and parked cars. The war official's spacecraft altered into a large robot after he selected a special setting on his control pad. This automaton grew even more massive than its original form and ten times stronger. Now that it was upgraded, it could go thirty-five percent faster than its regular pace.

"I never thought I'd have to move to drastic measures, but here I go. Let's play a little game, shall we?"

"What the heck is that?" Zella asked.

"Prepare for impact!" Vanilla screamed.

The monstrous hand of the malicious fiend opened up and a destructive red ray released from its palm shattering asteroids to fragments and smashed their space car to pieces. The two friends floated in space like bubbles because the yellowish orange clouds contained no gravitational force that kept them from falling directly down. They were terrified but extremely grateful to survive the blast. The buff mechanical machine obtained Zella in its fist and flew away.

"Let's have a little field trip! See if you can stop me now, dog!" The sinister commander chuckled as he headed in the opposite direction.

"Help! He's got me!"

"Zella, hang on!" Vanilla yelled as he endeavored to get a hold of himself from tumbling and turning about.

Vanilla did not know what to do. He would have transformed himself into a spaceship, but he hadn't reached that level of development. A small amount of trash started to float into his direction, after a heap of trash escaped from a garbage collector that swung by earlier. Within the dispersed clutter was a floating map that ran into him which had the directions and landmarks of the Zemustopeia territories. He took a cursory look at it.

After spotting a fatal swamp, the hero knew that the android was heading there. Vanilla had no choice but only to drift through the antigravity force. Although he was able to maintain full control of himself, the lack of gravity in that particular area of the clouds slowed him down drastically as he tried to direct himself.

Meanwhile, Zella struggled to break free out of the robot's clutch, but it was too robust to resist. She even tried using some of her verbal powers, but they did not make her situation any better. The young Zepulian recited some of her special sayings, but she was only able to slow the metal menace by only about five percent at most. She watched the massive sights of the cities pass by; the buildings and towers disappeared into the distance and the number of trees increased as they left the public zone. Up ahead, Zella took note of a sign that read:

> Warning: Do not enter.
> Going out of Zemustopeia Boundaries.
> Danger ahead!

Zella had a sense she was going to an atrocious place. A few hours later, the general in the unconventional combat ship entered the woodlands that led to the sweltering marsh.

"Zemus will be thrilled to hear the tragic ending of this hopeless protester's life!" He initiated the turbo drive.

Vanilla left the force of the chaotic atmosphere and began to tumble toward the ground. Luckily, the quick-thinking canine managed to shape-shifted into a piece of paper and the wind gently blew him in a calm breeze. In a few minutes, he found himself on the ground in a parking lot of a space car dealership. A skinny salesperson approached him in a hurry as if he was the only customer of the day.

"Hello!" said Vanilla still lightheaded from his preceding arrival.

"Hi, young fella. What can I do for ya today?"

"I need the fastest spacecraft you've got!"

"Sure thing, pal."

The sales man presented an exclusive model that accelerated to at least three-fourths of the robot's average velocity. The apprehensive client drew a bundle of multicolored plastic cards which had the five rulers' faces of the galaxy printed on them that were known as galactic dollars. Specific colors signified different values:

> Blue=1gd
> Orange=10gd
> Green=20gd
> Yellow=50gd
> Pink=100gd
> Red=500gd
> Purple=1000gd
> (Gd=galactic dollars)

When Vanilla reached the territory of timbers, it was becoming unnerving with quiet whispers and echoes. The determined dog heaved the turbo after he started to get frightened, trying his greatest to evade crashing into the tremendously tall trees.

Concurrently, Zella started to realize the trees vanishing as she grew nearer, the air became drier and warmer. The endangered hostage turned around to observe an enormous pit that was blazing with fury.

"This is it! Little girl, say good-bye!"

When the depraved military official made it to the destination, he stood over the scorching pool of death, and released his captive from his constricted grasp as she plunged to her doom. Vanilla's spaceship pulled out a large attached hand (one of the features for the newer prototypes) and caught her in nick of time.

"You've gotta be kidding me, right?" the boss roared. "There's no way that dumb dog could have survived that fall—and even if he did, he could never have made it back all the way over here in time! I will put an end to this foolishness once and for all!"

Highly frustrated, he tried to crush Vanilla's space car with his humongous hands and feet. As he made colossal holes and cracks in the ground, the floor rumbled with a few trees that fell over and were swallowed up by the sea of lava. After Vanilla got Zella safely in the compartment, he enervated the machine's legs with several quick blasts from his enhanced defense apparatuses causing the intimidating unit to collapse.

"What's happening? No! This can't be true! How could I be defeated by a pair of kids! No!"

The steel warrior descended into the blistering pond and the commander was incinerated as the wild waves of magma devoured the metal like an unfed army of termites.

"Thank you so much! I thought I was a goner!" Zella embraced her rescuer beyond standard gratitude.

"I thought you were too. Eh, it was no big deal! Let's get outta here. What a day, huh?"

"Tell me about it," Zella concurred. "Still, our adventure isn't over yet . . . we've still got some spying to do."

After another narrow escape, the victorious pair soared back to the Zemustopeia area. They remained at an inn in King Zemus's neighborhood and intended to watch him for the following days in his distrustful activity.

CHAPTER 4

The Journey Continues

Zorax, Zempunella, and Zork finally approached their subsequent stop in Zorgatto. This current world resembled a desert much as it was desiccated, barren, and burning hot. The buildings were mostly made of brick, and sand covered the sidewalks, with thirsty palm trees drooping over them. There was barely a single cloud in the sunset orange sky; their unfortunate absence was the reason to the unbearable heat, the traveling trio supposed.

"Can you believe the temperature on this planet? It makes me wanna just . . . give up and . . . turn back home!" Zempunella said, fanning herself.

"Yeah, what she said!" Zork added, panting.

"We're gonna have to bear it until we can find the next sensei's house." Zorax wiped a shower of sweat from his face.

The hikers spotted a barefooted youngster pushing a convenience cart that was three times his size.

"Come get your Zogo berry fruit smoothies for a galactic dollar! Would you guys like to buy some of my fresh cold drinks? Come on, it's really cheap and they're really tasty!

Especially when you're out in the sun all day!" he announced hyperactively.

He had bright red skin, light blue eyes, short dark brown hair, with a white and yellow colored cap on his head, a thin blue sleeveless cotton t-shirt, white silk shorts, and walked barefooted amongst the warm sandy terrain. Considering his appearance, it was reasonable to infer that he did not come from one of the richest families and was doing this to help his family in their financial struggle.

"Ah, I'm sorry, little champ, but we just don't have any money on us right now." Zorax knelt down and patted the minor vendor on his head.

"Aw, man! That's okay. Thanks anyway." The saddened youngster sluggishly turned away.

"He was so cute!" Zempunella said. "I feel so sorry for him."

"I wish there was something else we could have done for the little guy." Zork stated.

A few moments later, the Zorgolians overheard a scream from behind. When they spun around, the boy they had encountered before was running down the hill after his cart. The small stand was heading for a busy intersection, taunting the chasing child as it created more distance between them.

"No! My cart!" The little lad struggled to catch up with it.

"Come on, we have to help him," Zorax said, approaching the situation with this comrades.

The heedless kid ran into the risky roadway after his runaway wagon. As he approached the middle of the road, a drunken driver sped between the young boy and his barrow and cut him off unfeelingly, leaving a huge cloud of dust. The young citizen fell to his knees, coughing, incapable of getting up.

Another zooming vehicle swerved around the corner a block away. It seemed to be filled with a remote group of teenagers. Even though they couldn't see clearly, they continued to drive recklessly.

The cart stopped a few feet away from the boy, but he was still in danger of being hit. The car was within a few feet of him. Zempunella jumped in front of the boy, faced the progressing automobile, and held out her two hands with a high level of concentration as her antennae recurred in shining. A purple force field appeared and acted as a shield for her and the endangered civilian. The vehicle bounced back and fell over on its side with everyone okay.

Zorax jumped into the center of the crossway as well and used his telekinesis to push the road obstacle that the boy recently dashed for as it rolled across to the other side of the street safely before getting run over by a supply truck.

Zork lifted the boy and carried him to safety next to his supply carrier. Zorax and Zempunella followed him.

"Whew! That was close! You all right, kid?"

"Yeah, what were you thinking?" Zorax asked.

"Don't you ever do that again! Do you hear me? You could have gotten killed out there!" Zempunella said sounding like a worried sick mother.

"I'm sorry, guys. I didn't mean to put you through all this trouble. But you saved me and my cart! I think I owe you guys one . . . here! Take these smoothies as a free gift!"

"Oh no, we couldn't," Zorax said. "It wouldn't be right."

"No really! Please! I want you guys to have them!"

"Fine," Zorax said, "But promise us you'll be careful from now on."

"You got it!" The boy looked under his cart. "Oh no. You gotta be kidding me!"

"What's the matter?" Zork asked.

"The ice in my cooler melted!"

"I can fix that!" Zorax pointed his hands at the wooden box. A mystical frost arose from inside the chiller and a huge pile of ice cubes appeared.

"Wow cool, thanks! How'd you do that? I didn't know you were a superhero!"

"I wouldn't call it that, but you're welcome!"

"Thanks a lot, mister!" The kid ran off with his cart.

"See ya!" Zorax shouted.

"Good luck selling!" Zork said.

"Bye! Sweetie pie, be safe!" Zempunella added.

The following sensei brother's courtyard was a quarter of a mile away. The journeying teens sauntered down the tiring streets determined to reach their endpoint before nightfall. The sky began to darken and the stars started to twinkle in the distance of the chilly night.

"We're finally in the neighborhood!" Zork said with a mild sense of accomplishment in his voice.

"Yeah, but I wish we didn't arrive at night. It's kinda creepy," said Zempunella inspecting her surroundings very meticulously as if she were in a horror film.

"We just gotta find the next sensei before it gets any darker." Zorax looked ahead at the noiseless streets.

As they made their way through town, the vigilant posse heard an abrupt eruption of petrifying screams. They competed around the corner and to their horrendous surprise, gazed in tremor at an apartment building engulfed in flames, producing puffs of toxic smoke. Some inhabitants waited for emergency officials to arrive who appeared to be running late.

"Whoa! That is some fire!" Zempunella remarked frozen in fear.

"I know that face!" said Zork glancing over at Zorax, "You're crazy! You're not actually thinking about going in there, right?"

"We can't just sit here and wait for their mayor to send the rescue team over here. Let's get moving," Zorax exclaimed bolting towards the fire as if it were benign.

"Here we go again."

"Yep, there's really no stopping him, is there?"

People were shouting that there two toddlers were trapped on the third floor. Without any more contemplating, Zorax and the others made their way into the demolishing structure to repossess the children for their troubled parents. The intense heat on their faces caused them to sweat uncontrollably as do athletes at a gym; anyone else would have burned up, but Zorax used his aquatic capabilities to put out the conflagration in their path. On the third level, they discovered the children bawling and hiding under a crooked crib that was close to collapsing.

"There they are! Aw . . . don't cry guys. We're here to help!" Zempunella said content to know they were all right.

"Nice work, guys," said Zorax. "We're halfway done!"

"I'm starting to wonder what was worse—coming in here to start with or trying to get out of this place!" said Zork with a sensation of boundless doubt.

Zempunella and Zork each took a petite Zorgattoin in their cradling arms meanwhile Zorax concentrated on trying to ward off the fire. It was so out of control that he couldn't hinder it with water. Squeezing his eyes shut and focusing as firm as he could, Zorax enclosed the roasting apartment with dense coatings of ice inside and out. Amazed once again, as were his friends, at his talent to do this, so much that they would have stopped in wonderment if they hadn't been in haste.

"I'm not even gonna ask," Zempunella said dazed.

There was no time to think about it. He and his friends ran downstairs to return the younglings to their thankful guardians.

"Thank you so much," a woman in a purple nightgown exclaimed, shaking their hands and embracing her rescued children.

"There must be some way we can repay you kids!" her husband added.

"Oh, don't worry about it, sir! It's what we do!" Zempunella specified.

"Yeah, it was no big deal!" Zork guaranteed.

"Really, you sure?"

"We're good, thanks! Have a good night!" Zorax said with a wave, starting in the contrasting direction.

The benevolent set disappeared into the distance and continued their intermittent excursion alongside the road.

At the second quarter time setting of the third moon (9:30), the three voyagers knocked on the door of the sensei's household. Zorax stepped back, hearing footsteps approaching the door from the other side.

"Hello! How can I help you?"

"Hi, I'm Zorax, and this is my friend Zork and my sister Zempunella. Sorry to disturb you this late, but I was sent here by Zemo to train with you."

"Yes. Why didn't you say so! Come in, I'm Zamboni."

"Pleasure to meet you."

"We'll start tomorrow," Zamboni replied. "It's important to get a good night's rest first. I'll show you guys the guest bedrooms!"

Zamboni was a bit taller, older, and stronger than Zemo. He was in his early forties with red scaly skin and light green eyes with two long antennas. He had sandy orange hair and wore a long orange gown with big brown sandals.

Zorax and his friends spent the night in the guest bedrooms of the dojo. The next morning, Zorax scurried downstairs to train while Zempunella and Zork decided to tour the metropolis.

Zorax's training session was to acquire how to use fire, the fiercest element of them all. The scope was similar to a meditation area. Zamboni had set up a huge block of ice stuck solidly in a pot, which reminded his new student of the act he had performed earlier. Zorax's challenge was to liquefy the ice by boiling it.

"I know this may seem absurd at first, but you'll get the hang of it," Zamboni said. "Zemo tells me you're a fast learner."

"But that was ice, which isn't nearly as difficult as mastering fire."

"Let's not make any quick assumptions, my young friend. Any element or skill—and even problems that we encounter in life—will have the same level of difficulty. It just depends on the way we look at them."

"All right . . . if you say so," Zorax humbly accepted his given wisdom.

"Good, now close your eyes and concentrate," said the sensei, sipping a glass of steamy moon milk tea, which had the most savoring aroma that it nearly restricted Zorax's application.

As had happened before, the first couple of times Zorax struggled to complete his task.

"Let go of all the negative thoughts that give you frustration and clear your mind and only then you will be able to achieve this commission."

"I'm trying!" Zorax said growing a little intolerant.

The third time was different. His antenna began to flicker a dull shade of ginger, small flames appeared under the pot, and the ice quickly liquefied.

Zorax, peeking with one eye, was astounded as he saw what he had accomplished. In the corner of his eye, he saw his teacher shaking his head impressed.

Once the ice had melted, the liquid product started to evaporate promptly with bubbles appearing all over the surface, boiling like the rumble of a volcano. Zamboni tested the temperature by placing his hand in the water as if it were a thermometer. To Zorax's amazement, his educator did not pull back his inserted palm from the steaming pot in any fleetness but slowly retained it there until he received a reasonable estimate.

"Wow, job well done. It's come to approximately 2,000 sun doses (115 degrees) in less than ten seconds!"

"Is that good?"

"That's great!"

"You were right, it wasn't all that bad. I just had to focus a little more!"

"See I knew you could do it. Personally, I think fire is more fun to learn than ice, but don't tell Zemo I said that."

Zamboni clarified that when Zorax executed various powers, his antennae would gleam a definite color. The colors themselves were determined by the different powers.

A week later, Zorax and his pals said farewell to the additional tutor. They arranged their ship's coordinates to the fourth planet of the galaxy division. Zork browsed over the maps and guides he had accessible for details about locations and proposals for traveling.

As Zorax was flying the space car, a blinding light beamed through the rearview mirror. As the object came into vision, the young alien noticed it was a shooting star. Before Zorax could elude it, the star bashed their roving Z.U.V. off the marked thoroughfare.

"Hang on, guys!" Zorax shouted bracing himself once more as this very moment was only recurrent.

"Oh great, not again!" Zempunella complained, shortly overlooking the peril.

Screaming, the aliens wrestled with the gearshifts to get themselves back on the highway, but had no luck. After endless wrong turns, they found themselves completely alone with no indication of life anywhere.

"That was fun." Zorax got up from his hitting his head while falling. "Right, guys?"

"Fun? You almost killed us! What were you thinking?" Zempunella disputed.

"Well, my fault for not having unrealistic reflexes to something that's traveling at the speed of light!"

"Great! Now we're in the middle of nowhere and I have to listen you two go back and forth like there's no tomorrow!" said Zork full of sarcasm as usual.

"If someone could drive more carefully, then maybe we wouldn't be in this whole mess!" Zempunella continued the quarrel.

"Me! You're the one who—"

"Um guys," Zork interjected. "As much as I'd love to sit back and hear this senseless argument play out until eternity, I suggest you might wanna draw your attention towards that vortex that we're currently headed for."

"Va-va-vortex!" Zorax said.

"What is that?" Zempunella asked, her attention immediately seized, "It's huge!"

"I don't really wanna find out so can we get it moving pretty soon?" said Zork having the skill to say something nonchalantly that pertained serious matter. "Haven't we *almost* been killed by enough things already?"

"Don't just sit there and stare off into space while we're in space, Zorax! Turn this thing around. Hurry!" Zempunella frantically ordered.

"What do you think I'm trying to do? These dumb controls aren't even responding! Looks like we're stuck; it's too late!"

"So this how we finally die, huh? Get killed by a black hole thingy?" said Zork. "Talk about déjà vu."

The unmarked vortex sucked them up like a forceful tractor beam. The impact caused them momentary unconsciousness, but the whirling mass did not cause death—it only dealt with teleportation.

They awakened in the presence of a milky way. The galaxy of stars shone like polished diamonds in the darkness of space. Their ship drifted freely throughout the exposed expanse as they fully came back to their senses.

"We're not dead—that's a relief!" Zork said observing the new setting they were forcibly transmitted to.

"What happened? How come we're still alive?" Zempunella said.

"Wasn't that thing supposed to take us out for good?" Zork inputted.

"That *thing* probably wasn't as malignant as we thought it was—maybe it was one of those conveyance thingamajigs we read about last year in science," Zorax presumed.

"Right . . . those things. Whatever it was didn't kill us so I'm happy!" Zempunella acknowledged.

"Does anyone else notice there's like a bazillion stars out here?" Zork stunned.

"Yep, we must be in a milky way or something," Zorax answered.

"Okay, now that I know!" Zempunella finally recognized something.

The scientists of Zorga had remarkably discovered that shooting stars, gems, and just about any form of gold combined would upsurge the speed of a spacecraft when thrown in the engine tank. Zorax used his telepathic skills to make a shooting star come to him, struggling to diminish its pressure and rapidity as it came closer. When the star came to his hand, it distorted to fit his palm. The heroes stowed the desirable space matter in the motor with protective galactic gloves, which they had on before they ventured to initiate their diminutive mission.

After a few hours, Zempunella referred to the map and alerted the others of a forthcoming asteroid belt. Zork was cognizant that there were treasurable jewels inside rare asteroids. Zorax and Zempunella wandered how they would examine all these space rocks as they entered the throng of floating boulders. A brilliant thought popped into Zork's head that involved expending his special gift as his facial expression lit up with buoyancy. Instantly, Zork's antennae glared a lime green and generated four hundred replicas of himself. Before reproducing himself, Zork dressed his fists in a pair of galactic gloves again, which were also convenient in breaking through rough entities.

"Now it's my turn!" Zork exclaimed thrilled to show off what his capabilities.

Hurriedly, the cloned alien and his copies shattered the uncontrolled stones with energetic blows that drifted slowly like blown bubbles.

"Found some!" Copy 351 said.

Zempunella located the vibrant gemstones inside while Zork powered down to only himself again. The concluding piece to find was gold. To discover gold in the galaxy unit, the threesome had to catch a comet. A small corner store on a space island was the leading emblem of life they had seen for a while.

A welcoming stranger was marketing a couple of comet-catching mittens. They were usually immense, purple, and white made with a bloated cotton textile. The guy gave Zorax the brace for no charge and the pleased purchaser went out to the field where comets descended and fall deep into space.

"Now, I must warn you that these aren't regular comets. They're wicked fast! Their speed is off the charts!"

A rampant comet lurched toward him, but then swerved around Zorax. The second one was coming down fast and close, but he still missed. The hero could not cheat his way with his telekinesis because of the hustle of the comet. Finally, the superhero caught the comet in his right hand and was now overwhelmed with euphoria.

"Perfect!" Zorax remarked, glad his little session of embarrassment was finished.

The mittens exceled with an outstanding sparkle and the comet miraculously transformed to dust. When the dust cleared, the pursuers could not believe their eyes. It was a mound of gold coins as the closing product afore their staggered faces.

"Talk about extraterrestrial nature. These comets aren't normal."

"It looks like we're done here!"

The effective bunch set the glittery quantities in the apparatus of the interplanetary vehicle, waiting for a fruitful enhancement. Cooperatively, the motor began to drone vigorously and the sum of fuel was quadrupled as well would be the hover car's rate when it was put to the test.

"It looks like we're back in business, guys!" Zorax shouted awestruck.

"All right, back to square one—but at least we get a fresh start," Zempunella admitted. "Let's get a move on, boys!"

"Shouldn't we get some directions first?" Zork asked halting their rush.

"Good point. We wouldn't wanna end up like this again," Zorax replied. "Excuse me, sir, but do you know of any way to get back on the main roads?"

"Of course, young man. The simplest route would be to follow the trail of those stars to the end. They should get you right on back to the expressways or you could always go back and find that vortex that you said you popped out of if you prefer."

"Yeah . . . we'll take the milk way. Thanks!" Zempunella said certain not believing that he actually proposed that as a suggestion.

"All right, thanks!" Zorax climbed back into the ship and took off with his audacious partners.

They were going at a spectacular speed—good enough to save a few days of travel. The fourth world, Zigger-Zap, was not too distant now due to the fantastic upgrading.

CHAPTER 5

King Zemus's Wicked Plot

Vanilla and Zella concealed a micro-camera in King Zemus's lair to investigate further, knowing his every move. The two detectives viewed the king ordering his workforces to construct more spaceships. However, the complex machines weren't just ordinary transports, they were UFO's. UFO's in all galaxy units were prohibited since they were typically used for terrorist assaults. In addition, Zemus was in the procedure of duplicating his minions to form a military of thugs to strengthen his invasion. The vindictive general was in preparation to terrorize neighborhoods and towns throughout the sector.

King Zemus was avaricious and egocentric. This was the way he dealt with his anger in order to get what he wanted. He possessed the powers of ice, water, fire, telekinesis, lightning, flying, and many other abilities taught around the galaxy. No one had as much technique and uniqueness as him, and that's one of the reasons why he became so authoritative over the whole segment. After that, he started to discharge countless criminals out of confinement to do labor for him. Then he took over Zorgatopeia and turned it into Zemustopeia in honor of his name. This manipulating potentate would eradicate every living thing if he failed to obtain currency. It was vital for this collusion between him and his henchmen to be confidential because the attack was expected to be anonymous. The conniving villain's conspiracy was predicted to be complete in about one and a half weeks.

Vanilla and Zella managed to sneak in the dictator's manor. Encroaching in Zemus's mansion was everything but simple. He had at least twenty-one henchmen surrounding his entire home throughout the day. When the sly intruders got down to the basement, they sprinted for a miniature storage area at the termination of the corridor. Inside, the prying duo was revealed to limitless brown boxes parceled on shelves containing galactic explosives and other precarious munitions. They anticipated that Zemus was going to use them in the near future so they took action.

"What do you think he's gonna do with all these bombs sitting around? Who really needs this many for anything?" Zella questioned uneasily.

"I think I have a pretty good idea," said Vanilla as his eyes widened. "Come on! We gotta dispose of these things fast—before he does!"

"Right!" Zella corresponded with Vanilla following his lead.

A number not too far over from a dozen spaceships were built in the laboratory so far. Vanilla and Zella coincidently swiped exactly that many detonators from the packages and stuffed them in large dusty duffel bags. The explosives were plump and the magnitude of a tennis ball with a small timer in the middle. The pair dashed for the workroom, trying not to drop the particularly hefty masses. Zella used her abilities to make her-self indiscernible temporarily and relocated the fatal spheres into the assembled vessels. Vanilla took advantage of his exceptional knack of metamorphosis to make himself indistinguishable from a Zorogon lookout and told the others he was just inspecting. After the prosperous invaders sealed the metallic orbs on each ship, they proceeded gingerly and quickly.

"All right, let's get out of here before their suspicion gets worse!"

Vanilla and Zella scurried off the oppressor's turf before they engaged themselves in any more jeopardy.

Afterwards, King Zemus denounced a raging report on the local news that there had been a bomb-and-run crime. The anxious space sorcerer was so paranoid that he put up more security cameras, alarms, augmented the amount of his subordinates, and triplicated taxes on everything. He required all of his drudges and intellectual machines to sojourn and toil an even later night shift, and demanded twofold of their obligations. The revolting autocrat got into his scrutinized spacecraft, and flew off to a space island known as Zigabo.

Zigabo was a mere matter of insignificant land near ZiggerZap. The ZX6 landed near a forest on the little abandoned isle. It was a tropical environment with dangling palm trees and gorgeous springs. The breeze was tranquil and cool, and the sand and soil were moist. Zemus dictated his five soldiers who tagged along to hunt for outsized purple polka dotted eggs. Each troop snatched a gargantuan shell from the orange bushes, grunting because of its absurd heaviness.

"Hurry up, will ya! I don't have any patience left and time is flying by! I swear if even one of you slows me down today, none of you are getting paid at the end of this week—if I even consider paying you. Let's move it before I erase you all from existence!"

"Wow, the boss is really going crazy now, isn't he?" one of the bummed out collectors said to the other.

"Tell me about it. The guy is making us go Easter egg hunting for our punishment. What's up with that?" his associate replied on the same page.

"Foolish, simpleminded idiots. Once those offspring hatch, they'll realize how much I will no longer necessitate their assistance and how much powerful I will be. They'll witness and learn what true warriors are!" the deceitful warlord chuckled to himself.

As the hours went by, Zella followed the machination in action through another veiled viewing device that she had set on Zemus's ship previously. She witnessed an egg crack and a bulky avocado—colored beast emerging from it. Based on its brawny features it seemed to be extraordinarily stout and had the approximate height of a Zermamin Tree. (Average height of an NBA player)

The mysterious creatures that were hatching out of these eggs were called Ziggers. Ziggers were toned, broad-shouldered brutes that submitted to its hatcher's orders, which in this case was Zemus now. These monsters were nearly unbeatable to any force, and had tiny antennas on their bald heads. The menacing sovereign was planning to have a varied coalition of androids, Zorogon warriors, and Zigger progenies. Since his flying saucers had been sabotaged, rebuilding the project would take close to a month.

The next day arrived and the prior troublemakers entered the palace once more.

"Now we gotta be careful, Zella. After that little shenanigan that we pulled yesterday, they probably have patrol teams around this place like crazy!"

"Let's not stick around long enough to find out!" said Zella, tiptoeing with him.

In her skulking, Zella unintentionally treaded on a net and was captured by one of Zemus's new booby traps. A grating alarm reverberated as the sentries closed in on the two terrified trespassers. Vanilla hurtled away from the security guards as they pursued him out of the stronghold. One of the Ziggers with imposing agility abducted Zella, viciously conveying her to the central laboratory and presented the lurker to Zemus. Zella was flung on the cold hard floor anterior of the boss.

"Didn't I lock you up a couple weeks ago? Some people just don't learn their lesson, do they? I'll make sure your disruptive rebellions will be dealt with severely. Get her out of my sight immediately . . . Hold on just a minute, now that I think about it, there really is no possible way you could have gotten in and out of here so easily. Am I right?"

"What are you talking about? What's your point, you creep!"

"Don't play innocent and stupid with me, you lying little scum! You know exactly what I'm talking about. You'd have to possess some super ability or something in order to make your way around. Correct?"

Zella continued to stare at the ground as if she had never heard the question.

"You're speechless now, huh? Your refusal to cooperate will lead you to your own doom, you ignorant girl. Throw her in the power drainer!"

"No! Power drainer? You can't do that!" Zella fought the guards that tugged her away. "You'll never get away with this! My other friend was able to escape your clutches and he'll rescue me and expose your awful plot to the citizens of the galaxy unit!"

"There's another one of you brats?"

"Oops! I didn't just say that! But he's no real threat anyway so don't even bother trying."

"Silence! I will find him and destroy you both! I will send out a squad for his capture and tear down this whole galaxy if I have to! You meddling little morons have seen too much and I will not risk letting you ruin my hard work! You fool, because of your big mouth, you've put you and your friend's life more in jeopardy than to start with! Now take her away!"

The forceful Zigger hoisted the blameless Zepulian adolescent and tossed her in a body-sized glass tube that had cables and wires linked to another similar cylinder where Zemus put his enchanted conjurer staff inside to absorb the energy. The callous barbarian locked the poor prisoner inside and heaved back a small auburn lever. All of a sudden, Zella's vitality declined significantly, as she collapsed and her oral powers were completely withdrawn and transferred to the thieving ruler.

After depositing Zella's flair into his superior's rod, the compliant soldier brought the enfeebled dissident, who was now unconscious, to a detention cell. The demander had to use this shifting method to his power-containing shaft because he was not born with powers from his parents and those without congenital abilities were unable to grasp the opportunity to acquire new talents and skills. Therefore, he had to channel the source out of innocent victims in order to gain an abundance of strength.

Vanilla knew he had to unfetter Zella before doing anything else. Being separated from Zorax was enough.

The king's charmed pole consisted of a glossy crystal enclosed by a transparent sphere with a long polished golden pole joined from the bottom of the sphere about three feet in length. The purpose of having it was really for Zemus himself to attain a grand surplus of power. By using this wondrous knickknack, he was able to conserve the energy from his body that he initially placed in himself during a clash.

A couple days passed and Vanilla realized that the defense lines of Zemus's clutches grew exponentially. The space overlord eagerly awaited the presence of his intelligent enemy, however, running out of patience, sent some soldiers on foot, and ships after him.

weather. The atypical biosphere was suburban with tall gold leaf Zuzu berry trees and mountains. Zuzu berries were red and purple berries the size of grapes that were extremely sweet but vigorous and popular. The fruits are used in several best-selling smoothies and planted in various gardens and fields.

The subsequent morning, Zorax was asked to engender a thunderstorm—after grasping and developing the concept of this presented element. After innumerable disappointments, he gazed at the white clouds and pink sky, and meditated.

"Remember, just like fire, lightning is fierce. Make sure you are relaxed and focused."

"I think I got it this time!"

Eventually, the hero's antennae reflected a lively yellow light. During the fully focused attentiveness, the firmament turned white, and the clouds growled becoming gloomy, grayish, and substantial with tons of collected water droplets. Lightning followed with its incessant flashes in zigzags behind the mountains. Finally, rain trickled and drizzled on the boulevards and buildings all over the town.

"Yes, that's it. You've got the basics down. Very good."

The following night, Zork and Zempunella ambled from a respectable restaurant back to the hotel.

"That was some good food back there! We should visit there again before we leave," suggested Zempunella overwhelmed by its delightful service.

"Yeah totally, and the best part was that they gave us a discount on our food because we told them that we're new to town! It's a good thing that Zamboni gave us some money or we'd almost be broke."

They strolled down the sidewalk and took notice of a civilian not too far ahead.

A middle-aged aristocratic woman was waiting for a ride at the end of the block. The perfect target for a criminal, an unlawful scoundrel soon approached who aggressively confronted her. With a mighty tug, he was off with her classy handbag and scuttled through the vacant paths of the darkness as she shrieked completely caught off guard.

"Whoa! Please tell me you just saw that?" Zork remarked startled.

"Yep. Looks like we got some things to take care of!"

"They never give us a break, do they?"

They trailed after the bandit for six blocks, but the crook dashed into a shadowy passage.

"All right, hold it right there!" Zork commanded feeling like somewhat of a police officer.

The two city scouts had him cornered. He backed up against a tarnished ladder at the dead end brick wall. The felonious desperado ascended to escape, but he slipped yet caught his grip before falling. As Zork and Zempunella arrived on the roof of a corner store—where the ladder led—they beheld the fiend jump inside a space car that was sloppily parked, and flew off.

"Wow, he's a fast one, huh?" said Zempunella.

"Maybe we still have a chance to catch him. Let's head back to the ship," said Zork.

Later, they hopped in their Z.U.V. that was situated a couple of blocks north. They tracked the outlaw's ship for miles. The two crafts stylishly turned, twisted, and soared through the nighttime zephyr, avoiding flagpoles, office buildings, apartments, towers, and many other obstacles. It was out of the question to emanate any gunfire because of the lives that would be endangered in doing so.

"I hope this turns out well with all this fuel is costing us," said Zempunella.

"Just hold on. This shouldn't take very long as soon as I get a clean and clear shot."

Zork eyed and locked onto his objective. On a void block, Zork shot a fast laser at a streetlight, which fell and smashed into the getaway ship that the fugitive was in, knocking it out of control. The spacecraft spun around rapidly and crashed into a nearby alley, with smolder erupting into the perpendicular street. The purse-snatcher was hurled from his injured transport landing in a moldy trashcan.

"Gotcha!" Zork called out.

"Wow. Nice hit!" Zempunella said. "Took ya long enough."

Police detained the pest and telephoned the fire department to put out the flames before they were dispersed any further. The heroes gave the concerned women her purse and she acknowledged them with a wee black pouch of shiny pearls before getting in a taxi.

"Thanks again. You two kids are so brave and kind. That's the last time I come into an unknown neighborhood to have dinner this late at night!"

"If you do, make sure you're at least with a friend or something," Zork said.

"Nice meeting you," Zempunella added.

"Or at least learn a couple defense techniques," Zork mumbled.

"Shhh!" Zempunella elbowed him, trying not to laugh. "She almost heard you!"

"Another happy person thanks to us? Come on; let's get out of here before another purse snatcher comes up!" Zork said.

"I agree," Zempunella yawned moseyed alongside him.

The midnight was swallowed up by dawn, and Zorax had officially mastered the overall notion of how to conduct electricity. Zorgolaro handed Zorax an eye-catching silver medallion for good luck.

"You've come far, young one. You should be very proud of your hard work and progress!"

"Cool, thanks so much," said Zorax. "But, what is this for?"

"You will know fully soon in time, but for now, it is just a good luck charm."

"Sure—whatever you say."

As the evening settled in, Zorax waved good-bye as his friends and he prepared to leave Zigger-Zap.

"Thanks again, Zorgolaro!"

"Farewell, my friend. A safe and successful trip to you all!"

Zemustopeia was the next and last stop on their flight. Zorax, Zork, and Zempunella were off to the expressway. Taking this route would get them there in just about fourteen hours.

immense mound of rubbish. To his instant consternation and repulsion, he viewed a humongous life form consuming waste—as he began to move closer to the bottom by the potent creature. King Zemus's pet ate anything from vinegary milk to moldy bread and expired groceries. The hazardous gunk that the monstrous quadruped swallowed did not disturb him because his intestines were immune to it. The foreign organism possessed four dense extensive tentacles, sharp talons, and carnivorous fangs. The exposed scrap gave off such a putrid odor that Vanilla had to hold his breath.

This revolting life form was called a Zorgamon. This wild multiple-limbed critter desperately stretched for Vanilla to devour him whole. The petrified quarry attempted to shroud his self behind refuse cans and salvaging bins; however, the catastrophic killer lobbed them out of the way and focused on his appetizing prey. The adroit mutt hauled a lever on the wall, and a behemoth cage dropped and shut in the unctuous varmint. The massive leviathan bellowed in ire, knowing that he could no longer his desired victim.

"Whew! That was a close one!"

Vanilla slinked into the commodious garage around the corner. The incarcerated junk-eating hulk bayed, trying to get free.

Vanilla preserved himself out of sight behind a counter packed with gears when he spotted a twain of Ziggers take Zella into one of the gargantuan RR's (Rocket Racers). More than two hundred fifty battleships took off to cause gratuitous disorder. Fifty of the ships were headed to Zema in Zemustopeia and others in assemblies of the same quantity went to harass each planet.

Vanilla scrambled inside a space car and charged after the maneuvering commandos, but expressly for Zemus. The incursion was about to begin.

CHAPTER 8

Interplanetary Showdown

Zorax and his comrades at last turned up at Zema, Zemustopiea rambling along the walkways. When the cruising triple looked up, they detected the traitorous foray. Helpless commoners fled when city landmarks were spontaneously ambushed and caught on fire after sudden explosions.

"What the heck is going on?" Zempunella yelled.

"I don't know, but I have a feeling Zemus is behind it all," Zork predicted.

"Let's find out. We gotta get up there and stop those ships before they do any more damage! But while we're doing so, let's make sure to keep our eyes open for any sign of Vanilla."

"Right!"

The Zorgalian trine acquired distinct vehicles nigh a franchise—and came up with a blueprint. Conscious that the assailants were headed in multiple directions, Zempunella went to be the safeguard of Zepula, and Zork went to secure Zorga. Zorax took out his galactic communicator and called up Zemo, Zorgolaro, and Zamboni for some supplementary assistance. Zorax commenced firing at enemy lines, around a dozen shattered in clouds of conquest.

Zork navigated his space car to another grand vehicle supply department not too far away. The executive permitted Zork to borrow a couple dozen Zugazettes (commonly used ship model). Zork brought his imitation adroitness in to play and arranged thirty-six duplicates for the desolate ships. He and his reproductions went to skirmish with a more striking defense.

Zempunella modified her spacecraft to invisibility—along with herself—, which gave her an extraordinary asset contrary to fifty opponents.

Zella was detainee yet again in a warship that involved five Zorogon guards and three Ziggers directing its malign gunfire. She was located in scrappy lockup with white brick walls that contained a high amount of filth and cobwebs. Each rocket ship had an evidently marked digit on its lateral. If she could enlighten Vanilla on what divergent craft she was in, they might have a happenstance. When she looked at the wall in front of her cell, she saw a timeworn tapped paper covered in blotches.

1993
Spaceship Model
 # 025

Zella drew out her communicator that Zemus and his hoodlums were unacquainted of, and phoned her nomadic crony.

"Vanilla, you there? It's Zella!" she whispered.

"What's wrong? Are you okay?" Vanilla concerned.

"I'm fine, thanks. I think I may know a way you can find what ship I'm in. There should be a large number on the side of each ship. I think I'm in number twenty-five."

"All right, cool. Good thinking. Don't worry. I'll all be on the lookout!"

Vanilla had eliminated nearly two dozen adversaries by the time he ended the chat with Zella. He was grateful for the beneficial info knowing that he could have easily taken down her spaceship by misfortune.

Vanilla caught a glimpse of King Zemus's shuttle sheltered by the last five fighters. The dynamic pilot had taken out three-fifths of the sentinel ships with ease. One of the foe guardians bombarding wrathfully, annihilated Vanilla's tank engine. Agile in reflexes, he hit an emergency switch and withdrew in one piece in a minuscule emission pod. His galactic car collided into another troop's flyer, triggering a deleterious blast. The ulterior rival ship of the shielding band came expeditiously barraging after him as he wafted through space in his unprotected capsule. To make things worse, he was being sucked in by Zemusopeia's gravitational pull.

"Oh great! I've become the sitting space duck. I'm toast now!" Vanilla freaked.

An impulsive laser beam aimed at the side of the aggressor's ship that was closing in on him, straightaway reduced to smithereens. The unarmed hero fell through the atmosphere, screaming irrepressibly as his pod began to pick up serious speed.

Zemus had initiated his penetration with over two hundred spaceships, but only fifteen endured at this point. The once proud evildoer was mortified that his underlings had been overpowered so quickly and effortlessly. He hypothesized that Vanilla, Zella had something to do with the disappearance of his battleships, and as usual questioned how they could have possibly achieved such a large task alone. The king's spacecraft came to an immeasurable asteroid belt where he concealed his ship for fortification and a surprise attack on his competitors.

"Those troublesome two . . . just wait till they'll see what I have in store for them. They'll regret ever tampering with my mighty wrath!"

Vanilla reached the surface of Zemustopeia after being sucked into its atmosphere. He had transfigured his body into the form of a piece of paper for a tender landing unlike his pod, which had an appalling crash. He had to get back into the raging fight to deliver his new acquaintance. He was generously lent an auxiliary space car from a Zemustopeian citizen who seemed to have lost all hope but had special reserved faith in someone as courageous as him. In the galaxy, people habitually respected superheroes in their times of trouble—and offered any assistance.

Concomitantly, Zorax was persistently doing away with battleships as he made his way through the anarchy. Luckily for Zella, Zorax on no occasion came in contact with her ship.

All of Zorax's peers came back to Zemustopeia to help withstand the fleet of foes. In conclusion, all of the sky terrorists were eventually terminated. The six extraterrestrials came together in a space bus with tinted windows that the sensei brothers had provided. Its minor attached defense contrivances were sufficient to take out a middling opponent.

Zella's spaceship was finally hit and destroyed. She found herself in mid space out of the dismantled vessel, hearing the dismaying racket of a proximate war outburst. She was fortunate to escape the destruction, but was not certain how much longer she could subsist in her despair.

As usual, Vanilla appeared on time to answer the poor call of his colleague's distress and rescued her with another colossal red mechanical hand affixed to his stellar vehicle.

Now, the besetment was at last over. In due course, Vanilla, Zella, Zork, Zempunella, Zemo, Zorgolaro, and Zamboni came to the asteroid belt to defy Zemus.

"Vanilla! You're actually here!" Zempunella embraced her dog. "We've missed you buddy!"

"Where've ya been?" Zork said. "I see you've escaped Zemus's clutches at least."

"For now. We've been messing with Zemus and his guards. It's been fun! Sorry, I didn't call when I had the chance to," Vanilla said. "Zella and I have been exploring and kicking butt ever since we've met. She's been my traveling pal for a while."

"Oh hi, I'm Zempunella Zoomster. Nice to meet you."

"Zella Zinton, likewise."

"And I'm Zork Zitsu. And these are some of our new friends Zemo, Zamboni, and Zorgolaro. They were here to help out. They're skilled sensei who helped my friend Zorax train to fight Zemus."

The three brothers deferentially bowed to Zella and Vanilla.

"Now that everyone knows each other, let's get back to business," Vanilla said.

The crafty king activated a series of red and green buttons on his defense control pad and managed to fire at a cyclopean asteroid, causing many to tumble near the oppositionists.

"Whoa! Where'd that explosion come from?" Zempunella asked.

"Don't know, but I don't think all of Zemus's fighters were taken down . . . unless." Zella paused and took a gulp.

"Unless what?" Vanilla canvassed.

"You don't think it could be—" Zork said begging to catch onto Zella's thoughts.

"It's possible." Zella knew that Zork was reading her mind.

"In that case, we better act fast!" said Zork ready for action.

Zemo and he took the steering, maneuvering the blue levers forward, backward, left, and right. They sidestepped the forthcoming space rocks with spectacular dexterity showing no hesitation. Zamboni and Zorgolaro also aided by working together and used a blend of an electro-fire blast in order to disintegrate the incoming projectiles.

Zorax had just dropped in from his time-consuming trip from the blitzkrieg, taking notice and interest in the current situation. He was welcomed into the spacious shuttle when Zempunella opened a wide entrance for her brother to come in and join them.

Zemus whirled his magic staff in the air as small gusts of wind circled it rapidly and tiny snowflakes began to fall from it in gentle motion. After a couple spins of his wondrous wand, the sorcerer tested his technique on the distant freedom fighters. A light blue laser ray blasted out of the top of the rod, across the asteroid belt, and instantly made ruthless impact with the peacekeepers' bus. The shuttle curved and rotated out of control, bashing into few cruising boulders; everyone was thrown about recklessly.

When the recovering adventurers got to their feet, they realized in incredulity and slight gloom that their galactic transporter was completely frozen, buried by solid layers of ice. Every control and device in the ship failed to function.

"Great—the creep disabled the ship! Now what?" Zork grumbled with hopelessness.

Zorax rushed into the regulation room when he sensed the ship go numb after briskly parking his space car. He strode through the automatic entries and examined everyone's gape at the implausible powers of the sinister boss.

"What's going on?" Zorax broke the silence with his eagerness.

"He's captured us in some kinda ice chamber." Zella kindly informed introducing herself as Zorax suddenly became shy and blushed.

"Just face it," Zork said. "We're sitting ducks ready to be eliminated."

"Don't be so sure," Zamboni said, gesturing Zorax to assist him.

"What is it, master Zamboni?"

"Help me meditate in order to get rid of this hindrance." The master of fire said surely.

Zorax and Zamboni united their fire competences to thaw the ice while Zemus continued to launch rockets at a superfluous amount of asteroids, bringing about an even more daunting calamity.

"All right, who's got a plan?" Zorax requested open-minded.

"I might have one," a familiar voice proclaimed from behind.

Right away, Zorax paused and his application faded. He recognized that voice. He thought he was hallucinating, but the only way to find out was to turn around.

"Va . . . va . . . Vanilla!" wailed Zorax as he hurried over to his dog with the biggest bear hug he could give.

"Yup, it's me. The one and only," exclaimed Vanilla "Zorax, you're kinda killing me now. Can't really breathe!"

"Sorry. It's just that I can't believe you're actually here—and why didn't you say anything when you saw me come in?"

"Nothing's ever good without a little suspense, right?"

"I really hate to break up the reunion party, guys, but we should probably get back to reality while we're still a part of it," said Zork.

"Right, sorry." Zorax apologized a little embarrassed.

"I think I might have a plan, but I'm gonna need some of you to pitch in for it to work."

"What is it?" Zempunella said interestedly.

"All right, here's how it goes . . ."

When Zork withdrew from the ship, he succeeded in getting himself through the belt a couple meters in front of the king's ship, replicated himself a few dozen times, and became an impediment to Zemus's vision by overcrowding his windshield with several of the humongous rolling rocks. Zork and his genetic copies preoccupied him while Vanilla, who also left the space bus, was in pursuit of finding another asteroid, but in a much greater size.

"Ah! Get out of my way, you insolent irritations!" the king bellowed shaking his fist at the as they made taunting faces at him.

Zorax concentrated and transferred the asteroid that Vanilla had discovered—which was at least five times the normal capacity compared to the ones that Zork had gathered—and crashed it against the ZX6 with as much force he could give with the replicas fleeing at the last second before contact.

"Bingo!" Zorax exclaimed.

"Blasted! I can't stand those trifling kids. They messed up my expensive ship . . . Uh-oh What's going on? No! It can't be. How could they have possibly beaten me?" Zemus screeched in incomprehension, "This isn't the end!"

The controls and wires of the king's ship malfunctioned and his ship went crashing down, knocking into asteroids. The spaceship was dented and horribly smashed as it descended to Zemustopiea for an uncontrollable impact. Sparks flew off the dashboard and lights rapidly flashed while an emergency alarm buzzed in the background. Zemus chanted revengeful words at the successful heroes and warned them that they would soon regret messing up his plot.

Moments later, the cheerful caretakers of the galaxy unit maneuvered their spacecraft into the planet's atmosphere. They were approaching Zema, which was partially covered in heavy smoke and ferocious flames. Obnoxious noises emanated from citizens and emergency vehicles that rushed upon the scene.

When their traveling machine landed on ground floor in a parking lot a couple blocks away from the incident, they hurried to the scene. The ground was broken apart as if there had been an earthquake. Space cars and trucks were flipped over and streetlights, signs, and mailboxes were flung from the explosion and were wrecked to pieces. By the time most of the smoke cleared away and the fire was put out, the news crew surrounded the area, along with emergency teams that assisted injured Zemustopieans to the hospital.

Zemus's warship was crushed, destroyed, bruised, and covered in debris and dust. To his rivals' surprise, the defeated dictator slowly limped out of his ship onto the pavement and collapsed. His magic staff rolled a couple feet away from him. More emergency aliens arrived in a gliding space van and landed several yards away from the villain's unconscious body. These life forms looked bigger and stronger and meaner than the previous ones. They were dressed in blue and black shiny uniforms, assembled in a group of four, as they put the king's body in a long tube shaped pod. Next, they loaded the big transparent container into the back of their van, and blasted off back into the heights of the city.

The gang of good guys stood in amazement that they had actually taken down one of the most powerful beings in the universe, but they felt guilty about causing the town so much damage. They offered the help clean up for the rest of the day. However, it took no longer than two to three hours because they worked together and used their powers skillfully to get the job done quicker.

A few hours passed, and the law enforcement of the galaxy unit arrested Zemus and took him to jail after his medical treatment was finished. All the nations were infuriated and voted for a new leader immediately.

"I will get my revenge! That's one thing I'll make sure off!"

Later, the rest of Zemus's powers were drained at the prison area so he would not have a chance to break out. The ex-ruler was sentenced to jail for life and was not able to see any visitors whatsoever.

During the cleanup of Zema, Zella found the golden rod at the curb of the torn up pathway. As she picked it up, the powerful tool glowed and shook rapidly as an energetic flow of power surged into her arm and throughout her body. She felt like herself again when her powers returned. She dropped the sorcerer's stick; as it hit the ground, it shattered into thousands of pieces and disappeared with a flash of bright light.

Good had overcome evil once again!

CHAPTER 9

Reunited

Everyone gathered into the space bus as they went back to Zorga, impressed with their achievement, as Zorax welcomed Vanilla back with some his favorite snacks.

When the group arrived at Zorga, there was an extraordinary celebration. Many people provided gifts and presents from all over the galaxy unit—some gave money. Zorgatopolis cheered and praised the heroes. Several high-ranking officials were there to greet and welcome the honored warriors at a giant banquet downtown. The Zorgalians were celebrities—and they were placed in the city and galaxy unit's hall of fame. The grateful mayor awarded the team members pure golden medals and wrote a fantastic article about them and their good deeds. The article was published throughout the Zaybonnioso Galaxy in every paper, magazine, and catalog possible.

Meanwhile, officers also rearrested all the guards and thugs at Zemus's mansion and continued to search the large facility for anything suspicious. The police did not notice numerous Zigger eggs that were beginning to crack open in the basement.

PART 2

CHAPTER 10

Jail Breakout

Zorax and Vanilla were watching intergalactic trivia very late into the night. Zorax could not stop thinking about King Zemus breaking out of jail. If he did, what would be his next evil plan to get revenge? He tried to relax as he reached for a cool zerbert soda in the fridge, and went back to sit on the sofa with his dog.

Meanwhile, Zemus was offered the privilege of one call, and this call was to the Ziggers in his basement. He spoke almost inaudibly so the police officers would not overhear him. He told the Ziggers to break him out of prison—and to take the fastest spaceship in the manor.

"This is your chief who is speaking to you, my newborn beasts. Listen to the task I have for you."

"Speak and it shall be done, my lord."

"I need to make your way over to this detention facility immediately. Show them I'm not someone to play with!"

"As you wish, master. We won't be long."

The Zigger hung up the phone. Four creatures accepted their mission, started up the spacecraft, and blasted off to the Zorgatopolis Prison Department which was one of the best confinement centers there was in the galaxy unit.

Near the second half of the shining Zelspar moon, Zemus was in his cell, waiting for his hoodlums to rescue him. While he waited, he thought of ways to make Zorax's life very despondent.

"I can't believe I allowed those pesky brats to interrupt my brilliant works in motion. The worst thing is that there are more of them than just that dumb dog and that naive girl. That boy—the one who finished the amateur attack against me—I felt his energy over all the rest as if . . . he must be their leader of the group. Those two before are not the threat—he is! That's it. I will make him suffer until I break him down completely and then their little kiddy force that they pathetically put together will vanish faster than a shooting star!"

The Ziggers' ship arrived right before midnight. The minions decimated the security—coded door with their powerhouse might; it flew off and knocked three police guards in different directions. Five more officers started shooting; as they backed against the walls, the fearless foes came closer, indestructible to the bullets.

"I thought we had a security system for this place!"

"We don't anymore!"

"Hold it right there. Get down now on your knees!"

"How are we supposed to stop them? They're practically invulnerable!"

"We can't let them get to the cells! It's obvious that's where they're heading!"

One of the muscular beasts picked up a pair of guards and slammed them to the floor. Another one's antennae glowed gold—his muscles became stronger and bigger—and he punched a constable through the wall. Bricks crumbled to the floor and dust filled the air. The last two officers began to run, as the brutish raiders came after them.

One of the craven guards ran in a custodian closet and set the door in what he thought would be an inaccessible way by initiating the security lock. The other one maladroitly stumbled over a chair from a nearby table crashing mercilessly to the floor. A Zigger captured the innocent and lumbering official, threw him against the wall, and crushed him with his foot. The wild warriors ransacked the place by throwing tables over, smashing chairs, and destroying anything in their way.

The last sheriff knew his other coworkers were surely deceased. Hearing the ruckus and last screams from his fellow comrades, he pulled out a small walkie talkie and contacted the ZBI.

"Hello, hello! Can anyone hear me? This is officer Zingo at the Zorgatapolis Prison Department. I need help fast! There's been a break in! Hello?"

When he heard the angry life form coming closer, he panicked. The barbaric soldier busted the door down, slowly cornered his target, stared down on him with his cold eyes, raised his wide fist, and smashed the helpless officer through the floor. The terrible thugs dismantled all the security cameras and alarms that would detected them along their desperate search. Since their boss's cell was on the underground floor, they rushed down the staircase.

When they arrived at their master's lockup, they ripped the titanium bars in half like paper.

"What took you so long? I suppose it doesn't matter. Just get me out of here so I can start planning my revenge!"

Other jailers stood against the cell wall as the gang made their getaway. The masterminds boarded the spaceship and took off to Zeliustopeia. Before, Zeliustopiea was Zemustopiea, but after King Zemus's arrest, the planet name was changed. Now a sympathetic and lavish king, Zelius, has taken command.

The next morning, the intergalactic news reported the expiry of eight police officers and Zemus's enigmatic breakout. Zorax was startled and hurried up the stairs to his sister's room. Zempunella was gone, but he recalled that she had gone on a stroll throughout the park. When Zorax went to Zork's house, he had disappeared too.

Oddly, his best friend's front door was wide open and one of his windows was cracked open. Zorax investigated the house, found shattered glass, and defiled furniture as if a tornado had swept through.

"Zork, are you there? You left your front door open—at least I hope it was you. If this is a joke, it isn't funny. Hello? Anybody home?"

Upstairs, he saw a fragmented wooden railing and outsized holes in a couple of the steps. In Zork's bedroom, there was a cracked lamp lying on the carpeted floor and a tossed over dresser drawer, that seemed to be blocking the room door before, which was also flipped over on the ground. The daring detective looked down finding a note on Zork's bed that said . . .

> Dear Zorax Zoomster,
>
> My loyal Ziggers have captured your precious friend and sister! If you refuse to surrender, I will destroy your companions and continue to take away the loved ones of your life and then of course get rid of you permanently. See ya, superhero! At least I hope so—for your sake!

"Oh no, that dirty little dictator has them! He'll pay for this—especially if he hurts either one of them." said Zorax to himself with sudden rage.

Later, Zorax and Vanilla started the engine to the space car and headed to Zepula. When the two companions arrived, they explained to Zella about Zemus's threat and attempt.

"Wow. Really? I can't believe he came back so fast. It's only been two weeks since his arrest. This really isn't good," Zella remarked fretful.

"Here we go—another rescue mission. At least this time I get to be a part of the rescuing," said Vanilla.

"Let's get a move on while we still have time to make a rescue," said Zorax. "The question is how he broke out . . ."

Zella agreed to help her friends on the new journey, knowing the stakes were higher, but she was up for the challenge. The three chums were off to Zeliustopiea to commence a completely new venture.

CHAPTER 11

Zillozooba

Back at Zeliustopiea, Zork and Zempunella were held captive for a couple of agonizing hours. Zemus had moved to a lair that his friend had lent him in Zema from Zeris city, where he had previously lived, to hide from the probing detectives and police. Zemus's superior commander, Zillozooba, appeared on a big electronic screen in the laboratory.

"Hello, master," Zemus said bowing respectfully.

"Greetings, my worthy apprentice." Zillozooba replied.

Zillozooba was a mushi master and much powerful than King Zemus. He had light blue scaly skin, dark brown eyes, and his black cloak gave him a shadowy presence. Zillozooba was best known as a supreme space lord with vast combinations of powers that he had developed over a brief amount of time. Unlike Zemus, he contained the genes of natural power that were similar to Zella's—except he did not always have to speak in order to release it.

"If you want that cloning machine, you will hand over those prisoners. I could use a couple extra servants around here—or maybe even minions if they're worthy enough."

"Yes, my lord," Zemus answered compliant.

"See you in a few hours—and you better not be late."

Zemus was about to enter a different galaxy unit. The villain ordered two of his dependable Ziggers to take the two prisoners to the dungeon in the prepared spacecraft. The dutiful followers picked up Zempunella and Zork and took them away. Zillozooba did not have as many troops as Zemus did because he thought it was an unnecessary asset compared to the power he had. On other hand, while Zemus lived more on the side of fear. Although his boss did have a reasonable amount to keep his defense lines at a decent standard, it was true that he did not need it much.

Zillozooba lived in galaxy unit number two, (or the Zaybonnioso Galaxy sector B) when Zemus was in number one (or sector A). Zemus's supervisor possessed a great planet called Zoolaberg, where smugglers did secret illegal business. This wicked world was where all the ruthless crooks and thugs from all over the galaxy met. They committed crimes or plotted to become evil masterminds and dictate nations. Hundreds of space bases with thousands of henchmen were set up personally by this fiendish world-owning wizard. He had trainees and rookies at each base practicing to become the most vile, destructive soldiers that would eventually work alongside him or other villains.

Numerous asteroids, big blue and gray stars, and one great yellow moon, Zongo, surrounded Zoolaberg. The weather on this planet was cool and moist. The surface was mostly bulky rocky mountains and long paths of gravel, with polluted streams, and a few small, orange, thorny plants called Thornal bushes. These rare flowers contained strong, sweet nectar that is used in alcoholic beverages all over the area at secluded nightspots.

Meanwhile, Zorax, Vanilla, and Zella went down to the Zorgatapolis Prison Department. When they reached, they watched detectives scope the area like crazy, taking samples

When the law authorities finally approved, the tremendous trio strolled down the spooky prison halls. The cold cement floor seemed to be growing a fungus or mold, and the walls had splattered bloodstains with tiny purple insects running down them. After two flights of stairs and a couple turns, the group reached a large metal door that read: W 351.

"Well, here it is." Vanilla sighed.

The travelers stared at the entry, speculating what their next move would be—and who would be brave enough to take the next bold step.

"Let's not all go at once!" he said sarcastically, pushing an access card into a slot under the door handle.

The electronic pad signaled that the heavy door was now open—and a red bulb over the door turned green. Vanilla retrieved the card after the security system granted access.

"It's all you, bro!" Zempunella encouraged nervously.

"All right, guys. Wish me luck!" said Zorax, starting to regret his plan.

Zorax turned the silver handle and slowly stepped into the cell. When the criminals stared at them, the other two cowered behind him.

The huge prison room had steel bunk beds lined up orderly, three iron sinks attached to a white brick wall, a couple outdated metal urinals, and a small television hooked up on the top corner of a wall, with the most basic cable there was. The floor was exceedingly unsanitary with rotten gum spots, toenail clippings, food crumbs, and strewn clothing. There were at least a dozen and half or more to share the space.

Most of the imprisoned goons wore puffy yellow uniforms that stated their department and section of the jail. Others lazed in bed in their undergarments without a care of what was going on around them. The inmates—Zemus's Zorogon troops—were all between five and six feet, somewhat heavy built, and had small sharp horns. Their bodies were shaped like circles, with short legs and huge feet.

"Hello, guys," Zorax spinelessly whispered.

"Oh, look! It's the leader of the ones who put us in this dump. What could you possibly want?"

Many of the bitter mobsters jumped up and started to make a circle around the visitor. Some began to crack their knuckles and grind their teeth while others leaned against the wall and shot dirty looks at him. Zorax eased back in horror as they continued to progress on him.

The biggest Zorogon, who seemed to be the leader, made his way through the gathering, putting his large hands up indicating for everyone to stop. He seemed stronger than the rest and was definitely greater in size. He took a glimpse at Zorax, lowered his dark sunglasses, and turned back to his companions.

"Let the kid say what he has to say. Besides, if we beat him up, we'll be in here longer than we want."

Zorax was amazed on how fast the others backed down. When he noticed a tattoo on the left arm of the guy in big black and red letters that said *commander*, he understood why he had so much authority over them.

"Go ahead," the king of the cell, said.

Relieved that he wasn't attacked, Zorax cleared his throat and said, "I was just wondering if you could help me."

"Help you with what!" another brute barked.

When Zorax mentioned King Zemus, a lot of tension started building amongst the group of prisoners when one shouted . . .

"Zemus? That backstabbing, double-crossing traitor! I can't believe I ever agreed to work with him!"

"What happened?" Vanilla asked assuming it was safe to come in now.

"That two-faced, two-timing Zemus said that when the Ziggers broke in, they'd free us, but he lied and abandoned us here in the darkness!"

"You'll help us defeat him?" Zorax asked with a burst of sudden hopefulness.

"Why not, let's teach him a valuable lesson of his own medicine!"

The Zorogons agreed one hundred percent all the way.

After a serious discussion with the mayor and the police chief, Zorax, Vanilla, and Zella were able to free the convicts. Now, the group was almost ready for the trip to Zeliustopeia.

Zemus, four Ziggers, Zork, and Zempunella were approaching the second galaxy unit. At enormous golden gates that secured the outer rim of the new galaxy unit, two security guards requested identification. The general sent two of his reckless troops to massacre the gate passers.

Back at Zeliustopeia, Zorax, Zella, Vanilla, and fifteen troops arrived at Zemus's deserted fortress. The garage door required a password. After a Zorogon typed in the series of numbers—05921, the wide security door revealed a room full of cutting-edge ships. The troops split up into three squadrons. The eighteen journeyers went off to Zoolaberg with the necessary supplies and materials to save their friends.

Zemus parked his ship inside Zillozooba's lair. Zillozooba arrived with five Zorogon guards to greet his faithful apprentice. The four Ziggers stepped down with Zempunella, Zork, and their master. The boorish ogres flung the prisoners face-first on the ground. When Zillozooba snapped his fingers, two soldiers of his took the hostages away to a prison chamber. Another pair of henchmen carried a big cardboard box that was marked *Cloning Machine*. The Ziggers of Zemus positioned it thoughtfully in the ship.

"I guess I should warn you my commandant, that the medaling Zorax Zoomster will be lurking around the galaxy to stop our plans," Zemus said disgusted.

Zillozooba and Zemus entered the camera room with their warriors. The humongous room had an additional ten troopers securing the area. Each of the rooms in the lair was equipped with a standard security camera. The two harsh potentates sat down at a black, marble, and oval shaped table. Zillozooba ordered one of his privates to fetch two cups of blue Zerona tea, which was an herb mainly useful for energy throughout the day and the cleaning of internal organs.

"That worthless so-called hero," Zillozooba said. "I'll destroy him the minute I see him! He's no threat to me at all."

Zemus usually underestimated his boss's power; he didn't think Zillozooba had an idea of what he was up against.

A couple minutes later, Zemus and the Ziggers left, and made their way back to his current base.

As the search party proceeded through the halls, the sentinels began whispering among one another, and studied them as they walked by. Four patrolling Zorogons walked into the room where they saw the rescue squad had parked and found the departed troopers. The inspectors knew they had big trouble on their hands. They scurried into the unoccupied camera room, replayed the video footage—, and immediately sounded the alarm all over the extent.

"Quick—search this station from top to bottom! Call for reinforcements immediately! We have unwelcomed guests! Find them before it's too late—or we'll all be punished by Zooba's wrath!"

The alarm screeched around the station, causing distress and chaos. The posse doubled their efforts to find their companions, realizing there would not be much time until they were chased down.

"Okay, boys . . . and kids . . . we gotta get it moving now! Our plan has been terminated and it's time to fight!" the captain instructed.

"All right, guys, this is where the action starts. Get ready!" Zorax said to Zella and Vanilla.

When they got to the end of the hallway, two station officers stood by a security door leading to the prison chambers. Zella froze the wardens—and Zorax melted them with his fire technique—but the gang needed a code to access the door.

"Do you see these guys?" one of the rescue Zorogons said. "They're pretty skilled for a bunch of kids."

"No kidding. No wonder they beat Zemus so easily." the other replied in agreement.

Vanilla heard more armed assailants coming around the corner of the hall—and notified his team associates.

"Come on guys, we've gotten too far to fail. I know one of you has an idea that can get us out of this mess."

"Maybe we should hide behind those barrels across the hall," Zella suggested.

"That's it! Good idea," Zorax said, hurrying over to the enormous containers.

"We're hiding?" Zella remarked confused.

"No," Zorax said, pointing to the hallway hazards. "Read the labels on these things."

"Explosives," The commander Zorogon grinned, "Pretty impressive."

"Are you out of your mind," Zella debated. "Those are bombs. I know you can play with fire, but bombs?"

"If I'm so good with fire, I should have no problem keeping us safe when these big guys go off. I'm also an expert with water if this whole fire thing doesn't work out. So just relax, okay?"

"Whatever you say, Captain Zoomster," Zella replied rolling her eyes.

He unleashed his telekinesis to stack up the explosive barrels that the henchmen failed to finish storing away. After he warned his friends to stand back, his antennae shining red—fired a careful shot and wiped out the rangers with a deadly explosion that raged in the opposite direction. Zella used her special power to go through the brick walls, then once inside, she opened the door that blocked the rest of the group. As everyone else dashed around the corner, a pair of galactic robots defended the entry of the security door that led to Zork and Zempunella's compartment.

Galactic robots are small combat-trained war machines with rectangular heads and bright red antennas. They usually are built within a range of 4-5 feet and are equipped with laser cannons or defense gun blasters. The electronic warriors were named RZ's (Robots of Zillozooba) and usually had a label that indicated their brand and individual number. They were constructed mainly for the purpose of spying, which is why a portion of them are programmed with jetpacks, tape recorders, and other gadgets.

"How would you guys like a little tidal wave?" Zorax said as the robots prepared to fire.

He swept away the robots with a colossal wave that surged from his hands. He also used his lightning ability to extinguish the second door to bits revealing Zempunella and Zork sitting down against the wall full of boredom.

"Nice to see you guys!" Zork exclaimed happily. "How'd you find us?"

"Zorax, finally you came. I'm so glad you're here. I missed you." Zempunella hugged her older brother.

"You too. Now let's get out of here!"

The freed friends followed their courageous comrades through the vestibule, when they suddenly realized there was a massive cluster of Zorogon guards walking along with them. Zempunella walked over to Vanilla with curiosity and concern, with Zork behind her anxious for an answer too.

"Is it just me or are we walking with a group of Zoolamorian soldiers?" she whispered.

"Don't mind them. When Zemus dumped them, they kindly offered to help us take him and his boss down as payback."

"Awesome. They're on our side?" Zork came into the conversation with excitement.

"Yep. With these dudes and their amusing training experience and our terrific talents, we'll basically be unstoppable!"

Suddenly, the heroes felt the lair ground shaking and rumbling.

"Uh oh," Vanilla said. "That can't be good."

The space station was on its way in concluding in a drastic explosion, but there was no way everyone could make it to the rescue ships without making contact with the remaining sentries, fire, smoke, or deadly gases.

"Oh no, It looks like we got ourselves a code 112, boys!" the Zorogon captain stated. "I don't know if we'll have a successful ending."

"No! There's gotta be a way! We've gotten out of situations like this before," Zempunella said.

"She's right. We can't give up . . . but what are we supposed to do?" Vanilla deliberated.

"It's not like teamwork is gonna help us now," Zork said.

"But that's exactly what were gonna use," Zorax said. He remembered Zemo's words: *With the complete power of five or more, and much concentration, you all will master the power of minor teleportation!*

"I got it! We need to hold hands. I think I know a way to get out of here!"

"Wait . . . Seriously? How is holding hands gonna solve anything?" Zork questioned," You feeling okay, man?"

"What are ya trying to do here?" added Zempunella.

"Just do it! I don't have time to explain! Now!" Zorax grew impatient.

They joined hands and formed a circle around the fifteen troops. A blinding yellow light shined brightly over all the aliens and a force of energy teleported everybody to the mechanical section of the lair.

"Whoa, how'd you do that?" one of the Zorogons questioned in astonishment.

"When did you learn that?" Zella asked inquisitively.

"Never mind that," Zorax reminded. "We need to keep moving!"

"You heard the captain," the commander yelled. "Let's move!"

The station walls began to crumble and the ceilings began to collapse. Dust and debris filled the air, and evacuation warnings sounded over the intercom.

The team spotted a lime green jumbo space van, and briefly started the engine. Next, Zorax used the force from his telekinesis to open a large garage door that led to outer space, from inside the van, because it seemed to be jammed due to the discombobulating condition of the destroyed location. The heroes safely exited the base, and left the surrounding atmosphere at swift speed. About fifteen seconds later, the entire lair started to break down completely and the space station was incinerated instantly with the stranded guards inside

"Mission accomplished!" Vanilla shouted victoriously.

CHAPTER 13

Zelius versus Zemus

Zemus started with his new unethical plan to assemble a Zigger military. However, before following through, the envious despot sent three Ziggers to capture the new and approved King Zelius. As the minions went off to Zema—where Zelius lived—Zemus began to replicate the last Zigger.

The abundant Zorgalian bunch received an audiovisual message transferred from Princess Galaxious, the daughter of the new imperial leader.

"Salutations, fellow fighters. I need your help. I have a strong sense that my father is in danger, and that something bad is heading our direction fast. Do you think you can join us in defending our kingdom?"

"Of course, Your Excellency," Zorax confirmed. "We'll be there as soon as possible!"

"Thank you. I'll try helping the castle prepare for battle and emergency evacuation procedures, if needed, until your expected appearance."

"Looks like we got another mission on our hands," the Chief Zorogon said to Zorax.

"Yes, but this time it's more serious. We're dealing with royal officials now," Zorax replied.

"Don't worry. That's what we're here for." The commander loaded his blaster.

King Zelius sent some warriors to secure the castle perimeter from being too vulnerable and called the law enforcement headquarters to send more back up.

He had once been a normal Zorgalian citizen and was runner-up behind Zemus in the 1990s election. His wife, Zampoda Zelius, died in a disastrous spaceship accident a couple years before he took an interest in politics. He took over where Zemus left off—with his teenage daughter at his side. Immediately after he took over, he lowered taxes and rebuilt the destruction that Zemus caused while he was in power.

Zabalor Zelius had light green skin, and was dressed in a fluffy blue gown with yellow buttons. He wore a red bowtie and a large gold crown with red, blue, and green encrusted gems inside, which covered his baldhead. His outstanding outfit was finished with polished brown dress shoes and thin red velvet gloves. Since he took his occupation very seriously, he had little time to focus on his inherited power, which was the skill to release laser beams out of his hands.

Princess Galaxious looked forward to being a great leader like her dad one day. Galaxious was born in a faraway place known as the Gorgonix Galaxy, which is why her name begins with a G. She had turquoise skin and wore a hot pink bowtie on her head that complemented her long hair and her pink and blue antennas. Her white blouse was sewed together with a puffy pink dress. An elegant blue diamond necklace matched her silk gloves. To top that off, she completed her wardrobe high heeled boots with silver buttons. Besides her expertise in fashion, Galaxious possessed a set of odd powers that she has been practicing for a while, to defend herself for a reasonable amount of time.

The uninvited Ziggers landed in front of the palace a half an hour later. The castle guards charged with swords as the enemies stepped out of the shadows of their ship. The fearless foes from the arriving spaceship took the swords and bent them like a pencil in half. The gargantuan gatecrashers chucked the castle guardians through the brick walls of the invaded palace as if they were simply paper airplanes.

"I can't believe it! Do my eyes deceive me? Those creatures possess unbelievable strength! They are everything but normal, how's that even possible?" King Zelius exclaimed in horror.

"Come on, Dad. We have to get out of here while we still can!" his daughter panicked alongside him, leading the way.

They sprinted up to the regal transport, knowing it was too late to wait for assistance. The Ziggers marched up the stairs, making sure not to fail their mission.

"Come on! We must get them before they escape! They must not and will not get away so easily!" One of the trespassing troops remarked.

Galaxious used her special fog power to create a pinkish mist in the hallway, causing the creatures that were initially after them to smash into walls totally blinded by the thickness. As a result, the hunters decided to turn back from the ploy.

"That should keep them off our backs for a little while," the princess assumed, catching up with her dad.

King Zelius called for the Royal Spaceship Protection Program Company. The corporation, whose job it is to enforce the safety of royal leaders, immediately sent five combatant ships to aid the King and his daughter.

"Of course we are. Now cheer up, buddy. We still got a job to finish! Just gotta keep strong!" Zork said to Zorax giving him a friendly nudge.

"Your friends are correct. If we wanna stop Zemus in time, we must stay focused and keep moving. Remember to never give up. No matter how tough things may seem in life, you must continue to stride and use every obstacle and sorrow to give you strength along your way." The commander added.

"Right . . . thanks, Captain." Zorax appreciated.

"Call me Zink." He replied with a warm smile.

"You got it . . . Okay guys, let's go!" the team leader agreed to continue.

After the shock of the accident, the rest of the rescue group searched for miles through the opaque fog that covered the atmosphere. The heroes needed to get back to Zeliustopeia to hinder Zemus's diabolical plot. However, they had no idea where they were—or where they were headed.

CHAPTER 14

The Misty City of Zelabell

After eyeing their convenient guide, the progressive Zorgalians realized that they were in the territory of the Misty City of Zelabell. Zelabell was a small populated planet, but mostly peaceful and quiet, except for the Misty City. The Misty City was a ghost town jam-packed with criminals, trashed streets, cold nights, and deserted apartment buildings. The heroes had planned to take the train to the shuttle station to continue their interrupted trip.

"We may have lost some noble members, but we have to put our emotions aside and finish what we started," Zink reminded.

"Where are we? I can barely see with this dumb fog in the way!" Zella complained.

"I can fix that," Galaxious insisted.

She closed her eyes as her antennas glowed pink, held her hands out, and concentrated for a few moments. Slowly but surely, the mist cleared, moving to the side as if it were being gusted by a hefty fan.

"Nice work," said King Zelius impressed and then turning to Vanilla. "May I ask you why we are walking with criminals? We aren't hostages, are we?"

"No, but it's a long story," Vanilla sighed.

"Eh . . . Right," Zelius replied unsatisfied.

When they arrived at the surprisingly calm train station a couple miles southeast of the incident, they purchased tickets for the evening express train ride.

Eventually, the long public transportation vehicle approached the station. The train was made up off five separate compartments. Each boarding passenger of the pack acquired any available seat noticing the inside was virtually full. The order was, Zorax and Zork in the first, Vanilla and Zempunella in the second, Zella in the fourth, and King Zelius, Princess Galaxious, and the seven troops in the fifth.

The grey and green express departed from the Misty City to Zurtherama. The local carriage maneuvered effortlessly with style through the heavy vapor hitch. Zorax wondered how the engineer could drive without seeing anything. Nevertheless, the public transportation chauffeurs were used to it, and practiced a great deal throughout the year.

"Good evening, passengers. Thank you for joining us today and choosing MCZ transportation. I hope you enjoy the ride. We should be arriving in Zurtherama in a couple hours. Please find one of our traveling attendants if you have any personal requests, questions, or concerns."

However, a half an hour into the ride, the train driver lost his agile navigation when he accidently knocked over his mug of hot moon milk, and the panels and controls of the train became unresponsive and started to shut down.

"Oh no, you have got to be kidding me! Not now! Oh boy, come on, work, you stupid controls! Oh dear . . . this isn't good!" the clumsy driver freaked taking a deep swallow.

The elongated vehicle started to go out of control right before it was about to approach a bridge. The bulky brick bridge was perfectly arched over a dazzling sapphire colored spring lake. As the engineer pulled the half-broken brake lever, the train swayed to the left. The last train cars crashed off the end of the bridge, hanging over the edge, dangling above the gigantic lake, suspended in midair.

Innocent people were thrown all around as screams roared through the aisles of the scared to death riders. It was time for the heroes to get to work, with another grand disaster occurring with even higher stakes.

The first two train cars were on the train track safely, but the third was halfway off. The fourth and fifth train cars were off completely—and were on the verge of falling directly into the lake.

Zorax, Vanilla, Zork, and Zempunella—in the first and second train cars—broke the glass with Zorax's forceful electricity power, and went to handle the situation.

"We have to move fast," Zork shouted, "if we want to get everybody on safe ground."

Suddenly, the fifth train car fell, breaking from the fourth, and descended toward the lake—with Zelius, Galaxious, seven Zorogon soldiers, and five other passengers. Zorax used his telekinesis to bring the car back up, but the car's weight was too much. The coach was wobbling and shaking, caught between Zorax's ability and gravity.

"I can't hold this by myself . . . it's too big!" Zorax said his voice straining as he struggled.

"Hold on. I think I can help!" Zork suggested.

Zork produced five replicas of his self and hopped into Zorax's energy force. Now, Zork and his copies were floating in midair because of Zorax's telekinesis. The Zork copies picked up the train car with their collective strength, and Zorax led them prudently on the side of the track.

"Thanks. That was a great idea!" Zorax said relieved.

"No problem—but we still gotta help the others." Zork responded glad to help but aware their troubles were not over.

Next, Zorax directed the travelers in the rescued train car to step back as he shattered the rectangle windows with his outrageous lightning skills once more. The unfettered commuters came out of the compartment overjoyed, but still in shock.

Much like déjà vu, the fourth train car started to wobble and shake, and then plummeted in the direction of the murky river. Galaxious took advantage of her mystical talents and trapped the falling train car safely in an oversized bubble. It floated back up, landing near the previously rescued and detached train car.

"There we go!" she exclaimed successfully.

During the rescues, the train driver screamed, "Help! There's a train coming. I'm stuck!"

The driver's car was on another track—and another train was coming at an unstoppable speed.

Zorax elevated the driver's car with his psychic force, and the other train passed through with no physical contact, letting it gently down on the correct side of the track. The driver was tremendously grateful and the passengers applauded the heroes with plentiful esteem.

"Really great teamwork out there," the engineer complimented the hardworking helpers. "Boy, if we didn't have you kids on our train, who knows what horrible things would've happened today."

"Wow," Zelius said impressed again. "Another job well done."

Surprisingly, the train engineer's antennae and hands shined a color near violet—and he reassembled the train from all its broken components and loose material and set them back into well working machinery. In forty-five minutes, the train was ready, and the ride continued. Zorax, Zella, and Galaxious used their various types of energy forces to move the haze away from the driver's view.

The community transporter pulled into the shuttle station toward the end of the day. To thank them for the brilliant and brave saving, the station officials provided the heroes with first-class space shuttle tickets. Unfortunately, the flights were delayed for several days due to extreme fog conditions.

"What a bummer," Galaxious reacted hopelessly.

"Don't give up so fast," a Zorogon trooper, said reaching into his blue travel pack. "I've got something that might work."

He pulled out a communicator and called King Zemus's main contact number, hoping he had not changed it since his move to the new location.

"Hey, Boss?" the troop said after getting a clear signal to his belligerent superior, as Zemus appeared on the small square screen seeming very irritated as usual.

"What do you want?"

"My squadron and I have captured the young and ignorant Zorax and his buddies right here at the Zurtherama train station!"

"Excellent, maybe you aren't so worthless after all. I will send reinforcements there at once."

"Thank you, my lord."

The screen on the tiny piece of technology lost connection and then went blank.

"Good thinking," Zempunella exclaimed. "Now will be able to reach our desired destination without any wait."

"Awesome job, but why didn't you do that earlier—like right after the crash?" asked Vanilla questioning the soldier's intelligence.

"What are ya trying to say, dog, that I'm slow or something?" the Zorogon said in a low intimidating voice, offended, pulling the Vanilla by his collar.

"Oh no. I was just asking cause . . . um . . . please don't hurt me."

The revolutionary freedom fighters decided to come up with a plot to make sure the seizure was convincing.

CHAPTER 15

Plan Back to Zeliustopeia

The eager travelers waited on the outside driveway of the deafening and hectic station. After a decent wait, a red and blue striped spaceship landed in the public territory where a pair of cloned Ziggers trooped out to greet the Zorogons.

"Well . . . What do we have here? Are these the troublemakers?" One of the threatening thugs questioned.

"Yes, we ran into them after we . . . uh . . . broke out of the prison a couple days ago . . . and um . . . ran into them at the park," Zink attempted his best misleading, scratching his head and hoping his pathetic lie would work.

"Good work. You guys go inside. We'll take care of them." said the other ruffian.

The minions grabbed the pretend prisoners as everyone entered the ship that lifted off to Zeliustopiea.

"Wow, I can't believe that worked!" Zella whispered over to Zempunella.

"You're right—but how long until these numskulls figure out what's going on?" Zempunella inquired.

During the trip, Zorax and his friends were locked in a prison chamber. The Zorogons stood behind the Ziggers, uneasy that they would discover their plan. Suddenly,

Zillozooba and Zemus appeared on a wide communication screen saying that the Zorogon soldiers were spies and had destroyed Zillozooba's lair.

"They're backstabbing imposters, you fool, eliminate them immediately." Zillozooba commanded furiously, and then left the screen.

"Listen, you disgraceful idiots. If you think you'll embarrass me if front of my boss and fail to complete this simple assignment, I will personally banish the both of you from existence—and you should expect no mercy this time!"

The two pilots, turned the moving ship on autopilot, and approached the Zorogons.

"You decided to lie to us, huh?" one of the muscle-bound monsters spoke with rage as he began to crack his knuckles and his neck.

"Let's make them regret trying to play us. You're nothing but rookies. Our strength is a hundred of times greater than your pathetic levels. You'd be showing complete stupidity if you even think you could take us on. It was a grave mistake in joining those lowlife losers. After we finish you off, we will wipe them out.

"We'll see about that!" yelled the captain. "Men, give it everything you've got! We're not going down without a fight!"

They began shooting, but the Ziggers were unbeatable, as the shots just bounced off their chests. One of the beasts picked up two defenseless Zorogons and slammed them against the wall. In the midst of shooting, a Zorogon warrior accidently hit and broke the self-destruct button with a blazing bullet.

"Oops! What did I just do?"

"You fools! You've activated the suicide bombing system, but it is you who will suffer this tragedy—not us!"

They forgot the combat and ran to a small room where a single space pod was located and evacuated the ship.

"See ya, suckers. You should thank us though. You'll get an instant death instead of a slow, painful one! Enjoy your last minutes of life!"

The puny pod's engine roared and the goons were disconnected and abandoned their despised double crossers to their doom.

The rest of the Zorgalian group had three minutes and twenty seven seconds until the detonation. Zorax as usual, implemented his gifted endowment to free his friends and himself. Two of the seven Zorogon guards were harshly battered and were slowly drifting away from the little life that was left in them. Zella as well, applied one of her Mushi skills by reciting special primeval Zepulian words to avert the ship from exploding with a reverse saying that was stated as . . .

"Reverzscisco inationous zimbodio"

As her antenna was brightened with a white light, the ticking time on the self-destructor was erased and the system became innocuous once more and the Zorgalians had received a free spaceship courtesy of the Zoolamorians (alliance of the villains).

"Well, that was easy," Zella said simply.

"Wow, how'd you do that? You must study hard to remember all those sayings, huh" Zork venerated.

"Not really. I only know a couple so far. It's not as easy as it looks," Zella admitted.

Zorax and Vanilla flew the spaceship back to Zemus's lair, and followed the navigation system that the escapers had unwisely left on while the rest of the team checked on the suffering militaries.

At the same time, the pair of Ziggers with the escape pod, entered Zeliustopiea and rushed to tell their boorish chiefs about the recent news. The unreliable creatures returned to the lab of the lair, and addressed Zemus and Zillozooba deferentially with a bow. Zemus rose up out of his chair, waiting for an encouraging report on their task.

"Well?" the royal general said impatiently.

"Well, what?" his Ziggers played senseless purposely.

"The prisoners, you imbeciles. Where are they?" their master became irked.

"The spacecraft was set to self-destruct by those scoundrels so we evacuated immediately, sir."

"Did the prisoners escape?"

"We're not sure."

"Go find out, you lazy, ignorant good for nothing nimrods!"

"Yes, boss!" they replied moving fast in fear.

The goons desperately searched for their targets, knowing that King Zemus would be merciless if they failed again to complete their duty.

The galaxy battlers were more than downhearted when they found out that the bruised troops had passed away. Sadly, only a third remained alive now. The piloting pals landed the spaceship in the garage of Zemus's station, which was oddly located in the clouds and because his guards from the control room, thinking it was one of their kind, due to recognition of the familiar ship that had left from the base earlier, allowed the rebels ingress. As soon as the squad got out, a Zorogon from the group accessed the unchanged code to a nearby security entry.

As soon as the wide double doors opened, three Ziggers stood in the way. Galaxious trapped the thugs inside a floating soapy sphere that was almost unbreakable in order for them to proceed down the hallway serenely.

"Okay, I don't know how, but we have to find out a way to take down this army—or we and the whole galaxy unit are doomed!" Vanilla determined.

"Yeah and fast, I don't how long my bubble will hold them off," Galaxious added.

Zemus alerted his armed forces to be on the lookout for intruders. The lair was secured with Zorogons, Ziggers, and well-programmed security robots.

Meanwhile, The bubble-trapped troops busted out with a hard punch, and the outraged barbarians sought for the invaders.

When the heroes zipped across the corner, they spotted two additional Ziggers and three Zorogons with guns walking toward them. They were cornered.

"Oh great—as if we didn't have enough trouble in our hands," said Zella. "How are we supposed to stop the big ones who are invincible?"

"She's right," Zork said. "We've lost."

"I wouldn't be so sure," said Galaxious.

Luckily, Galaxious successfully knotted up the weak Zorogons with her plant power. Thick green vines wrapped around the enemies like pythons. The captured crooks tried their greatest effort to break free, but the more they struggled, the harder it squeezed the life out of them.

"Wow! Where is everyone learning all these wicked techniques?" Zork enquired in fascination.

However, the unapproachable Ziggers were very close; therefore, they had to think fast another time. Zorax used his telekinesis to push the guards back a few feet to buy some time.

As the Ziggers stumbled to the floor, Galaxious set up a blockade of thick fog with her mysterious power, followed by Zorax making a wide wall of ice stopping the guards in that section of the station—avoiding any encounter or interference.

The advancing alliance apprehended they needed to split up to avoid being captured all at once. It would also be more efficient to move at a more reasonable pace.

"This is how we'll do it," Captain Zink directed. "Let's go!"

Group#1	Group#2
King Zelius	Zorax
Princess Galaxious	Zella
Vanilla	Zempunella
4 Zorogon guards	Zork
	Captain Zink

CHAPTER 16

Zeliustopeia War

Group one took wings A and C of the depot while team two covered wings B and D.

Wing A = north, Wing B = south, Wing C = east, and Wing D = west

One of the Zorogons with no trouble accessed a password to a sealed door in the first squad, revealing King Zemus lying back in his rotation chair sipping soda, while his ill-treated adherents worked madly around him.

There was a duplicating contraption in the process of making multiple Ziggers at an unbelievable speed. There were a little over five hundred prepared already.

"Can you believe this madman making all this mayhem?" Zelius yelled in incomprehension.

"Nice alliteration!" Vanilla laughed.

"Dad, be quiet before you—"

"Who are you calling a madman, you useless and unworthy understudy!"

"So . . . this is what a supreme leader does on his free time, huh? Laze around while his employees do all the work.

No wonder the nation voted you out the very first chance they got."

A pair of robots, a Zorogon soldier, and a Zigger steadily approached the uninvited guests.

"That's it! I have no time for this lousy lecture of yours! Get them! Once you're in my hands, I'll make sure my strongest and most vicious Ziggers rip you apart limb from limb!" the conniving creep screamed.

"Run!" one of the Zorogons of group one shouted.

Knowing that they had to retreat, team one fled back to the ship—and they zoomed off in search of team two.

Simultaneously, the additional collection of freedom fighters came across an enormous garage where Zillozooba was making his frantic escape. There was a Zorogon pilot warming up the getaway ship's engine because the Zelustopeia atmosphere was colder than usual during this time of year; a duo of Ziggers sheltered Zemus's boss in case of unexpected disruptions.

"Stop them!" Zillozooba ordered.

The brawny savages charged at the heroes, but Zorax zapped them with a high voltage of electricity, causing them to dramatically collapse to the floor.

"I knew I shouldn't have depended on those weak warriors to get the job done," said Zillozooba passed regular displeasure. "Guess I must take care of you myself!"

Within a blink of an eye, the offensive side of intruders were pushed by an extraordinarily strong force that sent them flying out of the room, tumbling through the hallway, and crashing into a brick wall. With that being taken care of, the head Zoolamorian leader dashed into his spaceship, taking off at light speed.

"Wow," a Zorogon apart of team said amazed. "He has that same moving object with his mind thingy ability that your friend does."

"You mean Zorax," Zella answered rolling her eyes.

"Yeah, except his power is like ten times greater!"

"You're right," Zempunella agreed getting off the ground. "I've never experienced someone with such extravagant power. Zemus was a piece of work, but this guy seemed to be at least fifty times stronger."

"Whoever he is—I hope we don't run into him again," Zork said dusting of his shirt.

"Let's not take him for granted. He could be a tremendous threat in our future—and a danger to our society," Zorax warned.

King Zemus vaulted into his ZX6 to look for the troublesome heroes.

The second squad spotted an army of robots charging after them, eventually surrounding them at the end of the hall. Suddenly, a nearby door opened to reveal the first group hovering at the opening. Before the automata could do any harm, the cornered fugitives jumped inside the escape vessel and blasted off with the others.

"Just in the nick of time, guys!" Zorax exclaimed allayed that was not his last stand.

"That was an epic fail!" Vanilla remarked with mixed emotions.

"I guess breaking into Zemus's headquarters is not as easy as it used to be," Zella giggled.

"Huh?" Zorax said confused, with everyone else giving Vanilla and Zella puzzled looks as well.

"It's an inside joke," said Vanilla smiling.

As the gang flew away from the space station into the outer atmosphere, there was a detected danger on the ship's alarm system. A red light flashed on the dashboard on the control table. When Zork looked through the back windows, a solar corona ejection had just been blasted off the sun's surface—and was headed toward them and Zemus's base. Everyone responded in utter trepidation of this murderous storm that was ready to challenge his or her lives. One of the Zorogon men pushed the turbo jet lever, increasing the speed of the spaceship to a remarkable degree.

"I didn't know there was a sun around here," said Zork staggered.

Zemus activated his accelerator, taking notice of the terrifying tempest in the distance. As it came blazing toward his ship, he quickly twisted and flipped his spacecraft, avoiding his doom. The storm headed for the space base, engulfing the lair, jamming the station's controls, signals, wires, and connections—and causing a serious malfunction. Within no time flat, the entire station blew apart in an atrocious explosion.

The calamitous storm with the fire and smoke united to vaporize the once powerful Zigger army. The flare-up continued, raging impatiently towards the heroes' ship with a severe fire compound. Zorax, Zella, and Galaxious struggled, but successfully pressed the sun storm back in the direction it originated with their amalgamated forte.

"Nice work, guys," Zella said.

"You too," Zorax replied. "Another problem solved."

"Thanks, but it wasn't easy to say the least," Galaxious replied moderately fatigued.

King Zelius and Zempunella saw an asteroid belt floating toward the rear of Zemus's spaceship, but he was too busy yelling at a few of his soldiers to notice it. The Zoolamorian apprentice only realized his life was in jeopardy when one of his henchmen pointed it out. It was too late—the oversized space rocks surrounded the frightened foe—and he was trapped and enclosed in the middle of it.

"Blasted," Zemus cried. "You buffoons, look what you've done!"

The corona ejection made fierce contact with the asteroids, ending with a destructive detonation, as asteroids set others off like underground mines.

"No!" Zemus chanted. "How could someone as mighty, powerful, and intelligent as me be this easily defeated? I was supposed to be the most magnificent apprentice that ever lived! This isn't over, Zorax Zoomster!"

After hearing the sound of King Zemus's loud and final shriek turn to a faded scream, the heroes knew that their rival was finally defeated. As the fire swallowed him, he disappeared in the dark smoke along with his ship.

"We did it!" Vanilla screamed. "We defeated Zemus!"

"I can't believe it," Zella said about to cry. "All our trials and tribulations finally led us to the goal that we worked so hard for."

"It's only been three weeks since school finished and summer started," Zork cheered. "We still have tons of time to celebrate and kick back!"

"Congratulations to you and your friends," King Zelius said, shaking Zorax's hand. "I've never seen so much confidence, bravery, determination, and teamwork in a group of teenagers in my life. You really will change the universe for the better. Keep up the good work."

"Thank you very much," Zorax said overjoyed.

Zempunella ran toward her brother and hugged him tightly.

"Finally," she rejoiced. "We won, Zor. We won."

"I know, Zemp." He wrapped his arms around her. "And we couldn't have done it without you offering to help at the very beginning."

"You were fantastic the whole way through, Zork!" Galaxious said. "Zempunella's told me all the wonderful things you've done for everyone!"

The princess leaned forward and kissed Zork on the cheek.

"It's no biggy," Zork blushed. "Just looking out for the innocent ones."

"After all I've been through with you and your buddies, I can say that was one of the most intense and impressive adventures I've ever been on in my life. I highly admire and respect you and your team. You guys are real troopers." Commander Zink commended.

"Thanks, but we owe the real thanks to you guys. If you hadn't agreed to help us and taken so many sacrifices, we would never have gotten as far as we did. We'll always remember you and your lost companions."

Next, also elated, the three sensei brothers appeared in a sudden flash of light and approached Zorax with smiles on their faces.

"Young apprentice, you surely have made your way to impressive heights since the last time we met. I can see you've grown much stronger and learned a couple important things on your way," Zemo stated.

"Really? What do you mean?"

"Learning that your determination and perseverance go a long way—and by taking this adventure, you understand the importance of friendship and the hard work of a team."

"To never give up and work toward something you believe in—and that you thought needed to be changed—even when things seemed impossible at certain points," said Zamboni.

"And you've witnessed how the love of money and power can corrupt a person, their life, and cause others to suffer. When someone doesn't remember where they come from and how their past gave them the success in their present lives, then their future will surely lead them to destruction," Zorgolaro added.

"It's hard to continue without remembering those things. Thank you again. I couldn't have gotten where I am today without your help and generosity."

"No. Thank you. I hope we cross paths with you again soon. Good luck to you all," Zemo said. The brothers bowed in veneration and disappeared the same way they arrived.

"Same to you."

Zella walked over to Zorax as things began settling down.

"Zel, what's wrong?"

"Nothing really. It's just that I feel kind of bad for putting you down all the time and not supporting you as a friend. I guess I was just afraid. I've never been on a journey as long and extreme as this . . . where . . . our lives would be in jeopardy every other hour of the day, so I'm sorry."

"It's fine. I did some pretty crazy stuff back there, but I did it for the safety of others. I didn't mean to make you feel endangered—in fact, that's the last thing I'd want anyone to feel around me. Thanks for coming on this wild ride with us. I really enjoyed your company."

"Thanks," Zella said. "I'd love to go on every single adventure with you guys—as long as it has a happy ending like this."

The new friends laughed as they watched the stars and planets go by. It was one of the greatest days in history. The victorious voyagers headed back to Zorga to celebrate their achievements.

CHAPTER 17

Zorgatopolis Celebration

The Zorgalians landed in the parking lot of the Zorgatopolis town square after a six-hour flight. Thousands of townspeople gathered from all over the galaxy unit to get a glimpse of the superstars that had saved them.

Zorax, Zork, Zempunella, Vanilla, Zella, the five loyal Zorogons, their commander, and the two royal leaders waved to and greeted the paparazzi and the press. After the crowd settled down, the humble celebrities were invited to a fancy celebration where the humble role models met famous city officials.

The town congratulated and praised the adventurous space companions on a job well done. The party was substantial and historic enough to be broadcasted on almost every channel.

After an inspiring speech from King Zelius in honor of the triumph, each participant in the space journey was called up to the stage and given a shiny gold medal of gratitude and appreciation. Zorax stepped up to the podium and gave a brief message to their fans.

"Citizens of the galaxy unit, we have gone through thick and thin, ups and downs, and have encountered the worst possible disasters you could think off. Why? Because we never gave up on what we believed in. We continued to work together even though it might mean sacrificing our lives in battle. We stayed strong, and even though we stumbled along the way, we stuck to our goal and kept on trying. That's what makes us successful! Keep in mind that we are still ordinary beings that took action for something that we thought needed to be changed for the good of the community. With that said, let us progress under the reign of the new Zelius Kingdom and become the desired nation we once were."

Zorax was elected top general of a new Zorgalian army of about twenty-five thousand troops. The five Zorogons and their bold senior officer became the top five officials that ran the drills and attacks and became the best teachers and tutors for their squadrons because the best skill was experience.

Various colored fireworks exploded in the sky spelling out . . . The victory of the Zorgalians and defeat of the Zoolamorians!

Two weeks later . . .

On a late evening, Zorax was playing fetch with Vanilla like always when Zorax pulled out his communicator as it rang gallingly in his left pocket.

"What's the matter, Zorax? Your throwing game has been off lately." Vanilla taunted.

"Whatever . . . uh . . . Hold on. I'm getting a message." Zorax replied preoccupied.

His old pal, Popcyn, required help to stop an overruling dictator who threatened his society in a faraway galaxy. Zorax called up a couple of familiar friends, and they began their trip to a new location.

"Here we go again," he said with a slight sigh.

Stuck and stranded on a planet called Zorina after a major crash, Zillozooba swore harsh retaliation to put an end to Zorax and his meddling friends, in honor of Zemus and himself—and he had the perfect plan in mind . . .

GLOSSARY

Dynamite Asteroid: An asteroid that contains an explosive chemical; it will detonate if it comes in contact with another object.

Galactic Communicator: A small rectangular high-tech device that can call, text, play music, record, take pictures, etc. They have small red and green buttons at the bottom and a square visual screen above. Also, they have a tiny gray extendable metal antenna attached at the top, for signaling purposes.

Galactic Glove: Galactic gloves are used to protect the hands of the user and can withstand almost any dangerous chemical, substance, or mixture that they may come in contact with when worn.

Galaxy Unit: A divided part of the galaxy, containing sections of grouped-together planets.

Highway/Main roads/ Expressway/ Speedway: A pathway of light that the majority of aliens follow while traveling through space that leads to every planet of the universe.

Space car/taxi: A vehicle that is made to drive on planet terrain and fly through space.

Space Island: A piece of land that stands firmly in the midst of space.

Sun Dose: A unit used to measure temperature in the Zayboniosso Galaxy.

Zellolonians: A system used to measure age.

Zema: The largest city in the galaxy unit.

Zerbert: A creamy substance used in drinks.

Zerona: A type of tea that grows from a plant in the second galaxy unit.

ZUV: A utility vehicle created in Zorgatapolis.

Zorgalians: The alien raise on the planet Zorga, also the alliance of Zorax and his comrades.

Zoolamorians: The Alliance of Zillozooba.